MY BIG FAT ZOMBIE GOLDFISH
THE SEAQUEL

WITHDRAWN

MO O'HARA
ILLUSTRATED BY MAREK JAGUCKI

FEIWEL AND FRIENDS
NEW YORK

A FEIWEL AND FRIENDS BOOK
An Imprint of Macmillan

MY BIG FAT ZOMBIE GOLDFISH: THE SEAQUEL. Text copyright © 2013 by
Mo O'Hara. Illustrations copyright © 2013 by Marek Jagucki.
All rights reserved. Printed in the United States of America by
R. R. Donnelley & Sons Company, Harrisonburg, Virginia.
For information, address Feiwel and Friends,
175 Fifth Avenue, New York, N.Y. 10010.

A CIP catalog record for this book is available from the British Library

ISBN: 978-1-250-02920-1 (hardcover) / 978-1-4668-5697-4 (ebook)

Feiwel and Friends logo designed by Filomena Tuosto

The poetry extract on page 119 is taken from "Trees" by Joyce Kilmer,
originally published in *Trees and Other Poems* by Joyce Kilmer by the
George H. Doran Company in 1914.

Originally published in the UK by Macmillan Children's Books,
a division of Macmillan Publishers Limited.

First published in the United States by Feiwel and Friends,
an imprint of Macmillan.

First U.S. Edition: 2014

10 9 8 7 6 5 4 3

mackids.com

THE MYSTERY OF THE ZOMBIE VACATION

CHAPTER 1

THE LONG AND WINDING ROAD

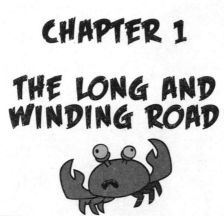

Pradeep looked even greener than Frankie's zombie goldfish eyes as we sat in the back of my dad's car. And every time Dad screeched round another bend, Pradeep turned a deeper shade of green. We were on our way to the vacation place that Dad had booked. Usually only Dad, my Evil Scientist big brother Mark, Pradeep's dad and his evil computer-genius big brother Sanj went on the Big Summer Weekend. But this year Sanj was at computer camp, and for the first time Dad said me and Pradeep were old enough to come. Nothing was going to wreck this weekend!

Not Pradeep, who was just about to hurl for the fifth time in four hours (I could tell because he had that surprised look on his face again). Not Sami, Pradeep's three-year-old sister, who had to come with us because as soon as our moms heard Pradeep and I were going away too, they booked themselves on a Massage and Mud Pack weekend. (Which I didn't understand at all. Moms hate mud on your shoes. They *really* hate mud on the living room carpet. But apparently they love it on their faces. Who knew?) This weekend wouldn't even be ruined by Mark not saying a word to me since he found out that Pradeep, Sami, and I were coming. If only he wouldn't thump me too, then it would be perfect.

"Bag," Pradeep mumbled as we went over a bump in the road.

"Bag," I said to Sami as she bounced in her car seat next to me. She passed me one of the stack of airplane sick bags that Pradeep's mom had packed for him for the journey. I unfolded it and passed it to Pradeep. Pradeep's mom gets these super-strong sick bags off the Internet because they can hold loads without breaking. They make the best splat bombs ever 'cause they never burst until they hit their target. It seemed a shame to waste them on actual car sickness. But a kid's gotta do what a kid's gotta do.

"Bleeech!" Pradeep filled the sick bag and then stared out the window.

"Are we there yet? Are we there yet?" Sami sang from her seat.

Dad looked straight ahead at the winding road. "About twenty minutes maybe," he said.

Pradeep's dad was looking at his smartphone. "It's 13.2 miles exactly to the destination." Pradeep's dad could get a job as one of those GPS things in cars. He's got the perfect voice for it. You would totally believe that he knew where he was going, even if he didn't. I don't think he would fit on the dashboard though.

"If you look toward the sea, you can see the lighthouse from here," Dad said.

Pradeep, Sami, and I all craned our necks to look. The lighthouse was tall and white like a swirly whipped vanilla ice-cream cone sticking up out of the sea. That is, if swirly whipped vanilla ice-cream cones had giant lights at the top of them. It jutted out into the bay so the water lapped against it.

Mark sat slumped in the back of the car behind us, flicking through *Evil Scientist* magazine. This month's cover feature was called "How to Take Over the World in Ten Easy Steps."

He had his earbuds in and didn't even look up when Dad spoke.

"It's awesome, Mark. An actual lighthouse," I said to him.

Mark shot me an evil glare. "There is nothing awesome about this moron-fest vacation." He pulled his hood up over his head. "You losers have made this the lamest trip ever."

The cooler that was under Sami's feet started shaking. I lifted the lid to investigate. The eyes of Frankie, my zombie goldfish, glowed green as he batted cans of Coke against the sides of the cooler with his fins. He must have heard Mark's voice and gone all zombie mega-thrash fish. He still held a grudge against my brother for trying to murder him with his Evil Scientist toxic gunk. Luckily, Pradeep and I shocked Frankie back to life with a battery, and ever since, he's been our friend and fishy bodyguard. I hoped Frankie would calm down soon.

"Swishy fish!" Sami shouted.

I put my finger to my lips and turned to Sami. "Shhhhhh!"

"What was that, precious?" asked Pradeep's dad.

"Uh, I think she's just excited about seeing fish in the sea," I said, covering for her.

Sami giggled and I carefully closed the lid of the cooler. Safe for now.

As Pradeep and I looked out the window, we saw a thick layer of fog hanging over the lighthouse, wrapping itself around a barely visible sign. I squinted to read it. WELCOME TO EEL BAY, it said in big letters, and then in smaller print that looked like it was painted on just yesterday, DON'T FEED THE EELS! ESPECIALLY THE EVIL ONE!

CHAPTER 2

THE EVIL EEL OF EEL BAY

Pradeep was still green, but he gave me a look that said, "That sign said there was an evil eel? Why is it everywhere we go there is something evil?" At the same time, his mouth was saying, "Next bag."

I totally understood the look and shot him one that said, "We so have to find out about that," while I passed him the bag. Who says kids can't multitask?

We pulled up outside the lighthouse just as it was starting to get dark. The beacon in the lighthouse tower glowed through the fog and made the place look like the set of some old scary movie. Goose bumps spread over my arms, and

I got that creepy feeling of millipedes wriggling awake in my stomach.

Pradeep looked less green as soon as he got out of the car. He unloaded the row of sick bags at his feet into the garbage can by the driveway. Sami jumped down and ran over to her dad.

"Want to see the sea!" she squealed.

"Not tonight, precious," Pradeep's dad said, scooping her up on to his shoulders. "Tomorrow the sea. Tonight—dinner, then bed."

Mark slid out of the car and looked around. "Stupid lighthouse." He looked at me and Pradeep. "Stupid morons. Stupid vacation."

I jumped out of the car, and Pradeep and I pulled out the cooler.

"Come on, Mark," Dad said. Dad hadn't figured out yet that trying to get Mark excited about anything that wasn't evil was basically a lost cause. "It'll be fun. We'll go fishing tomorrow."

The cooler started shaking again. I put my foot on it to try to stop it. It looked like I was tapping my foot to the beat of some random imaginary song.

"I, um, don't think I want to catch fish, Dad," I said.

"If you don't help catch them, you can't eat them. That's the rule on these vacations, isn't it, Mark?"

Mark nodded but glared. He was not going to forgive us for coming on his and Dad's annual weekend away.

"But I don't want to eat any fish," I said loud enough for Frankie to hear through the cooler.

"I've decided to become a pescatarian," Pradeep announced, "so I won't eat fish either."

"Pescatarians eat fish, but not other meat," Pradeep's dad said.

"Then I'll be whatever it is that doesn't eat fish," Pradeep said. "An anti-pescatarian?"

"OK. More fish for us then, right, Baskhar?" my dad said to Pradeep's father.

The cooler stopped shaking. Then I heard a

voice that made *me* start shaking.

"You the city folk then?" The gravelly mumble came from the doorway of the lighthouse.

A man stepped forward so we could see him. Or he stepped forward so he could see us better in the fading light. Or he stumbled out because one foot had decided that it would walk but hadn't got around to telling the other foot yet. I think it was mostly the third option.

This guy was definitely the oldest person I had *ever* seen. Older than Gran, older than the crossing guard we have to help us cross the street outside school, even older than that *really* old guy in that alien movie who spent light years in suspended animation. He was wearing a battered green raincoat that looked as if it could keep out a flood. His head was covered with a flat cap, and what showed of his face looked like one of those 3-D maps of deserts that they have in school, showing sand dunes where his chin should be.

I suddenly realized why he looked familiar and was just about to tell Pradeep when he shot me a look that said, "He's like a lighthouse keeper from a *Scooby-Doo* cartoon. At some point this weekend he has to say, 'I'd have gotten away with it too if it wasn't for you meddling kids!'"

I shot Pradeep a look that said, "YES!" and then one that said, "Hey, if he's the creepy bad guy, does that make us the meddling kids?"

"What's the matter? Cat got your tongue?" The ancient lighthouse keeper's voice cut through the fog like a pirate's rusty knife. He stared straight at Pradeep and me.

If this was a scary movie, this would be the point where you shout at the people in the movie to get back in their car and go home.

CHAPTER 3

THE OLD MAN OF THE SEA-QUEL

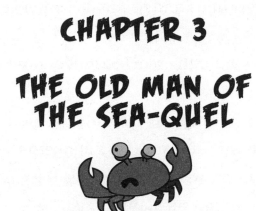

Pradeep opened his mouth. For a second I thought he was going to say, "If there was a cat hanging off my tongue, it probably would be hard to speak, not to mention very painful." Instead he said, "I'm Pradeep and this is Tom, Sami, and Mark." He smiled at the old man like he was talking to the head teacher in full trying-to-get-us-out-of-detention mode. That smarmy smirk is Pradeep's speciality. I don't know how many detentions he's got us out of with it, but it's gotta be in the hundreds.

"And I'm John and this is Baskhar," added Dad. The old man shook the dads' hands, then nodded over at us and grunted, "Better come in then."

"In the sea, in the sea!" Sami bounced on her dad's shoulders.

"There's no going in the water at night." The old man turned to Sami. "It's dangerous enough in the daytime, when you can see the eels . . . but at night they can sneak up on ya."

"Do you mean the evil eel?" I piped up.

"Where did you hear about the evil eel?" He spun around and glared at me. "Has word of the monster spread to the cities?"

"Um, it was on the sign coming in," Pradeep said. "So is it really evil or just mostly evil?"

Mark pulled his earbuds out of his ears. "There's an evil eel? Cool."

"It is not cool, young man," the lighthouse keeper growled. "It's evil and nasty and a danger to man and boat alike."

"Cool," Mark repeated, and put the earbuds back in.

The lighthouse keeper muttered something about "teenagers today" as we carried all our stuff into a large round living room at the bottom of the lighthouse.

As the lighthouse keeper stoked the fire, he told us more about the eel.

"A few months back the evil beast appeared. No one knows from where. He's the biggest eel ever to pass through these waters and has a jaw that can snap an oar in two."

"Surely that's an exaggeration," Pradeep's dad said, hugging Sami tightly as she sat on his lap.

The lighthouse keeper pulled out two pieces of an oar from under the couch. The thick wood had clearly been snapped by something with a huge mouth and lots of teeth. I decided that I didn't want to meet whatever did *that* to the oar.

"I'm sure he just tells these stories to keep the tourists interested," my dad said, ruffling my hair and giving me a look that either said, "Don't worry, sport!" or, "Yum, Spam for dinner!" (I'm not really up on reading my dad's looks, and the two are pretty similar.)

"I wish it *was* just some story made up to bamboozle the likes of wide-eyed landlubbers like you," the old man said. "But the truth is, it's kept most folk away. The monster keeps jumping out of the water, nearly capsizing the boats. People are scared to death of it. You're the

only tourists booked this summer. If someone doesn't catch that evil eel soon, that'll be it for this lighthouse and for Eel Bay."

Sami yawned and snuggled into her dad's shoulder.

"It looks like the little one is bored of all this talk about eels. So let's talk about dinner," said the old man with a grin. "On the menu tonight . . . is eel pie and green jelly."

Pradeep went green again and ran out the door.

CHAPTER 4

DOWNRIGHT DASTARDLY DEEDS

Pradeep and I threw our stuff on the bunk beds in our room near the top of the lighthouse. Then we opened the cooler and gave Frankie some food—green jelly that I'd snuck out from dinner. Being a zombie goldfish, Frankie eats only green food: mouldy bread, pond scum—the grosser the better.

As he gobbled up the green goo, we talked about the evil eel.

"Do you think an eel could really bite an oar in half like that?" I asked Pradeep.

"I've heard of conger eels that are over eight feet long," he said.

I tried stepping across the floor to measure that out. Then I gave up. "How big is that?" I asked.

"It could hang off the basketball hoops at school and still touch the floor," Pradeep answered.

I was trying to picture a mega-sized eel snapping an oar in two when we heard a stomping coming down the stairs.

Mark was in the room above us, Pradeep's dad and Sami were below us, and Dad was below them, next to the old lighthouse keeper's room. I saw his bedroom door when I helped Dad carry up the bags.

It had a big sign on it that said, NO MEDDLING KIDS! with a smaller sign nailed on top saying, EVER!

Mark stomped into the room without knocking, almost flattening Pradeep as he kicked open the door.

"Morons," he said, "you're not gonna wreck my vacation and you are not gonna wreck my evil plan. Got it?"

"We don't even know what your evil plan is, so how can we wreck it?" I said.

"You won't ever guess what it is, 'cause it's way too evil and sinister and . . . *dastardly*," Mark replied.

"Did you just use the word *dastardly* in real life?" Pradeep asked.

"It's the word of the day on the calendar that came free with *Evil Scientist* magazine." Mark scowled. "Anyway, it doesn't matter 'cause my evil plan to catch the evil eel is *so* secret . . ." He stopped and banged his palm against his forehead. "Look, just stay out of it. Or else!" He leaned over me menacingly and the millipedes in my stomach not only woke up but started having a party. This wasn't good.

Just as Mark was about to show Pradeep and me what he meant by "Or else!" Frankie jumped out of the cooler, whacked Mark across the face with his tail and flipped back into the chilly water.

"What the . . . ?" Mark stumbled back. "You

brought the moron goldfish!" Then he rubbed his hands together. "Even better. Now I can flush that stupid fish once and for all."

"No, wait!" I shouted. "If you leave Frankie alone, then we won't tell Dad that you're going to catch the evil eel." It wasn't the best deal, but it was all I could come up with at the time.

"We promise not to try to stop you, but maybe you should leave it alone, Mark," Pradeep said. "The eel could be dangerous."

Ever since he became an Evil Scientist when he got a chemistry set from our grandparents and tried to toxic-gunk Frankie to death, Mark has had the creepiest Evil Scientist laugh.

"You've got a deal, morons." He grinned. "Just keep the fish away from me, or he might end up as eel bait." Then he laughed his biggest Evil Scientist laugh *ever*, which in that creepy old lighthouse sounded off-the-chart scary: "Mwhahahahahahahahahaha!"

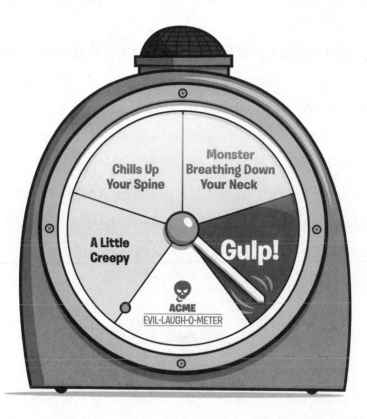

Frankie thrashed around in the cooler and glared his hypno-green stare at Mark. Normally, a stare like that would have someone hypnotized and under Frankie's control in a second, but Mark just stared back at him and grinned. "Ha! Patented Evil Scientist hypnotic-stare-repellent contact lenses, so don't even bother, fish!"

Then he strode out of the room and slammed the door.

Pradeep and I stared at the door for a second before either of us spoke.

"So, there's an evil eel out to get everybody, an Evil Scientist out to get the evil eel, and a zombie goldfish out to get the Evil Scientist," I said. "This vacation gets more like a *Scooby-Doo* episode every second."

CHAPTER 5

DO THE ZOMBIE-ZOMBIE SHAKE

The next day started with a *thud!* and an *ugh!*

The *thud!* was the sound of me rolling out of the top bunk and landing on the floor next to Pradeep, who had rolled out of his bunk too.

The *ugh!* was the sound I made as I got up and rubbed my head.

"Pradeep, what time is it?" I asked, shaking my head to wake up my brain.

I had got into the habit of morning brain shaking after a teacher told me once when I was at school that my brain was still asleep. I thought about it (obviously *after* my brain woke up) and realized he might be right. So I started shaking my head every day to make sure my brain was actually awake at important times.

I could hear Frankie sloshing around in his open cooler. "Morning, Frankie," I said. We had put the cooler right next to the radiator so Frankie could warm up a bit after being stuck in there with melting ice all day yesterday. I looked inside. Frankie was doing fin lifts with a can of cola.

Pradeep rolled over and opened his eyes. "Why am I on the floor? Where are we? Why are you shaking your head?" his look said.

"Obviously, I'm shaking my head to wake up my brain," my look replied. Out loud I said, "We're at the lighthouse, remember?"

Suddenly Pradeep jumped up. "We have to check out that eel before Mark gets to it."

"I've been thinking about that," I said. "The lighthouse keeper said that if someone doesn't catch that eel, he'll have to close the lighthouse. Mark would actually be helping him out." Then I interrupted myself, "Wait, Mark doesn't do anything to help anyone who's not evil. The lighthouse keeper seems pretty creepy, but do you think he's actually evil?"

"I don't think so," Pradeep replied, "but I also don't think Mark is catching the eel just to help him out. We need to figure out Mark's plan."

We put Frankie in one of Pradeep's sick bags, filled with water from the cooler, and carried him upstairs to Mark's room. We slowly creaked open the heavy wooden door and looked inside.

No Mark.

"Now we need to see if he left any clues," Pradeep said. He went over to Mark's suitcase and started searching in there. I went over to the table. Science goggles, earbuds, Evil Scientists-R-Us catalog. I picked it up and flicked to a page called "Ten Must-Have Evil Scientist Accessories." There at number one were the Evil Scientist hypnotic-stare-repellent contact lenses.

"I think I found something," called Pradeep, holding up Mark's white Evil Scientist coat and chemistry set. "Funny packing for a vacation!"

"Well, we did bring a fish," I replied.

Just then Frankie tipped the sick bag of water out onto Mark's desk. I grabbed a towel from the end of the bed. Frankie was flipping around on top of a piece of paper with something drawn on it.

Pradeep grabbed the sick bag and ran out to

the bathroom to refill it while I mopped up the spill. Pradeep was just about to scoop Frankie up to put him in the bag when we both noticed Frankie had stopped flopping around. Not in a "can't breathe" way, but in an "I'm reading the piece of paper" kind of way.

When did he learn how to do that?

CHAPTER 6

EVIL EQUATIONS AND SINISTER SKETCHES

Pradeep and I bent over the paper on Mark's desk. It was a diagram of some kind. There was a squiggly worm thing on one side of the paper and the lighthouse being hit by a big bolt of lightning on the opposite side. Mark had written *Mwhahahaha* coming out of the mouth of a little character dressed in a white Evil Scientist coat at the bottom of the page.

An arrow pointing to the squiggly thing had something else written above it, but it was too smudged to read from the water.

Pradeep plopped Frankie back into the water-filled sick bag as I spoke. "I don't know exactly

what he's planning, but I'm pretty sure that, as usual, it's evil. And that squiggly worm thing is probably . . ." I looked at Pradeep.

"The evil eel!" we said together. "We've gotta stop him."

We heard a motor *putt-putt*ing outside. We looked out the open window to see Mark heading out into the bay in the lighthouse motorboat.

"He's already out there!" I yelled to Pradeep. "Come on! Quick!"

We ran down the spiral stairs of the lighthouse, Frankie splashing against the sides of the sick bag. As we rounded the last corner, we ran straight into the lighthouse keeper, nearly knocking him over.

"No running in the lighthouse!" he shouted. "What in Eel Bay are you up to?"

He stared hard at both of us. Then his eyes moved to the sick bag in Pradeep's hands. "Seasick in a lighthouse? I've never heard of a landlubber so bad in all my years! Don't let me stop you." He motioned for us to pass him so Pradeep could get outside quickly.

Result! I knew that Pradeep's motion sickness would save the day one day.

Well, OK, I didn't actually know that, but it's pretty cool that it did.

We headed straight to the living room. The

dads were both there with cups of coffee next to them, texting and talking on their smartphones. "Looks like this is the only room in the house where there's any signal, boys," Dad said. "Some important work messages came in last night. I just need to sort a few things out."

"My boss has hit the roof over a misallocated *blah, blah, blah,*" Pradeep's dad said.

They had gone into business mode and I had tuned out. My brain translates lots of things—jelly-bean code, flag code, even Scooby-Doo's mumbling—but not business talk.

"How about we go out on one of the boats after lunch?" Dad said.

"Why don't you two go down to the beach for now and see who can find the biggest shell?" Pradeep's dad suggested. Pradeep gave him the standard "I am not a three-year-old girl" look. "Or the biggest, scariest crab?" his dad added.

"You can even try fishing from the beach

if you want," Dad said. The sick bag started shaking again.

Pradeep pretended it was him. "Excuse me, I gotta go!" he yelled as he dashed out with the bag.

"OK, Dad, we'll hit the beach," I said. "Hey, where's Sami?"

"She's sleeping late this morning," said Pradeep's dad. "The trip must have tired her out."

I ran outside and met Pradeep. "OK, we're good to go. Sami is asleep and the dads are plugged into their phones for the next couple of hours."

Pradeep walked over to the jetty, where a second boat was tied up. "Good," he said, "'cause look what I found. We can use this rowboat to follow Mark."

Now you might be thinking this isn't a great plan. Surely:

Pradeep + boat = lots of throwing up.

But it's weird—Pradeep gets sick in cars, buses, airplanes, roller coasters, and pretty much everything that moves, but the one place Pradeep doesn't get seasick is on the sea.

CHAPTER 7

NOT-SO-SMOOTH SAILING

Pradeep and I started to untie the boat. I brushed some seaweed off the side. "It's called *A Vision of Velma*," I said, reading the name that was painted there in swirly writing. "Hey, have you ever rowed a real boat before?"

"No, but how hard can it be?" Pradeep answered.

We slipped on some life jackets and put Frankie's sick bag in the bottom of the boat. Half an hour and four super-sore arms later I said, "Really, *really* hard."

We could see Mark up ahead of us, but it seemed to take ages to get close. He was in a

motorboat after all, and we were rowing.

Finally we got close enough to read the name on the side of Mark's boat. *Daphne's Delight,* it read in slanted writing. Mark had his back to us and was pulling hard on a long fishing rod, trying to reel something in.

"Do you think he caught the . . ." I started, but before I could finish, my question was answered by a mega-long eel leaping into the air alongside Mark's boat.

"Eeeeeeeeeeeeeeeel!" Pradeep and I both squealed. Now, I'm not a kid who squeals on a regular basis. Pradeep isn't either. I don't squeal at mice or spiders or scary movies or disgusting unidentifiable things stuck to the bottom of my sneaker. But I think that squealing when a massive eel jumps out of the water near you is fair enough. I dare you not to squeal if it happens to you!

Amazingly, Mark kept ahold of the fishing rod— but the motorboat rocked hard from

side to side. Then we heard a sound that none of us expected. Not Mark, not me, and especially not Pradeep.

"Naughty swishy eel!" a small voice shouted from Mark's boat.

We looked over to see Sami climbing out from under a tarpaulin in the bottom of *Daphne's Delight*. "I want to see sea. Not play with naughty eel!" she shouted as she stood up.

Mark nearly dropped the fishing rod. "Little moron?" he said, twisting around. "Were you hiding under there the whole time?"

Then he noticed me and Pradeep in the rowboat. "What is this? A *moron*-family outing?" he yelled.

Sami giggled and started singing, "Sami went to sea, sea, sea to see what she could see, see, see . . ."

At that moment the eel pulled hard on the line and it jerked the boat.

Sami wobbled back and forth for a moment, before a final rock of the boat sent her tumbling into the water.

CHAPTER 8
TUMBLING TODDLER TERROR

Mark looked too stunned to move.

"Sami!" Pradeep screamed and sprang into action. He grabbed a spare life jacket from the bottom of our boat and held it tight in his hand.

"Pradeep, wait! I'll get help!" I shouted.

"There's no time," he said, handing me his glasses. "I'm a good swimmer. I'm coming, Sami!" he yelled as he leaped into the choppy water.

The eel looked as if it was in pain. The hook hung out of its mouth and its eyes glared at Mark. It reared up and splashed down again and again, sending wave after wave of water

sloshing into both boats. If it kept on doing that, we'd all sink!

"Let go, Mark!" I yelled.

Pradeep had reached Sami and had her hanging on to the life jacket. He dragged her over to our boat and shoved her up so she could reach the side. I hauled her in and she slumped down into the well of the boat next to Frankie. She was soggy and shaken, but at least she was safe!

I held my hand over the side to help pull Pradeep in too.

That's when I saw a fin, then another fin, and then the tail. It whacked against the side of *A Vision of Velma*, knocking me over and shoving the boat out of Pradeep's reach. When I scrambled back to my feet, I could see that the evil eel was surrounding Pradeep.

"Look out!" I yelled.

Suddenly I saw a flash of orange fins and green eyes swoosh past me.

Frankie had leaped out of his bag and into the water. His eyes were pulsing with green zombie power as he flung himself toward Pradeep.

Sami stood up in our boat next to me. All I kept thinking was, "Come on, Frankie. Come on!"

Mark yanked on the fishing line again, which seemed to make the eel even more angry. It tightened its grip around Pradeep as he tried to swim back to our boat.

"Help!" Pradeep gasped as he struggled to keep his face above the water.

"Maybe the eel will go away if you just let go!" I screamed at Mark.

But Mark kept hold of the fishing rod. "Are

you nuts, moron? If I let go, then the eel can bite him too!"

The eel's head reared out of the water just by Pradeep. Sami clutched my hand.

The creature thrashed back and forth wildly, trying to loosen the hook stuck in its mouth.

Then I saw Frankie leap out of the water, right between Pradeep and the eel. Frankie's eyes were blazing green. For a second the eel seemed stunned by Frankie's zombie stare. Frankie almost seemed to hover in midair—you know, like ninjas do in fight scenes in those old kung fu movies.

The eel's eyes crossed and he looked at the boat with one eye and up Pradeep's left nostril with the other. Frankie had done it—he had hypnotized the eel! It loosened its coils and Pradeep pulled free. Just as he slipped out of its grip, the eel shook its head hard, like it was trying to wake up its brain and shake off Frankie's stare. Then it plunged back into the

water with Frankie close behind.

"Swim, Pradeep! Swim!" I urged him. He
quickly made it to the boat, and we pulled him
inside. Sami clung to the leg of his soggy jeans and
wouldn't let go. Pradeep shoved on his glasses
and peered over the side, looking for Frankie.

Mark called, "Get out of here, morons! Row
back to shore and leave the eel to me!"

"Where swishy fishy?" Sami shouted to Mark.

"That moron fish is eel food!" Mark yelled back. "If the eel hasn't eaten him already, I'll feed him to it myself."

CHAPTER 9

EEL BE COMING TO GET YOU

Mark got as far as the "Mwha" of his evil laugh when he was cut short by the evil eel leaping across the front of his boat. Then I saw a green glow approaching. Frankie was alive! My zombie goldfish jumped out of the water and managed to bash Mark with his tail fin as he passed. Mark dropped the rod as he tried to swat at Frankie. Frankie splashed back into the water, right into the waiting jaws of the eel! Its powerful mouth tried to clamp down on him, but Frankie pushed back just as hard—holding himself straight as a rod and propping open the evil eel's jaws.

"Naughty eel!" Sami shouted. "Let go, swishy fishy!"

Either the eel didn't care, didn't understand English, or didn't think she was talking to him, so it didn't stop trying to munch Frankie. Frankie's green eyes were bulging even more than normal as he strained to keep the eel's mouth from snapping shut.

"We've got to do something!" Pradeep yelled.

Then I spotted the sick bag still full of water in the bottom of our boat. I crumpled down the top of it so it was sealed up tight. One water bomb, ready to go. Then I pulled back my arm, ready to throw.

Now, I'm not the best pitcher in the world. My baseball career ended badly in third grade after a ball I threw hit the coach somewhere very painful between his knees and his middle. It wouldn't have been so bad, but he was standing over by the garbage cans at the time, nowhere near home plate.

The water bomb flew into the air and headed toward Mark's boat just as he grabbed his floating fishing rod out of the sea. The swishing rod flicked the water bomb back toward us, but luckily, Pradeep was ready with one of the oars. He batted the water bomb back toward the eel and hit it square on its head.

The evil eel dropped Frankie and turned toward us. In less than a second Frankie had leaped in the air and landed on the giant eel's nose. He stared a hard zombie stare right into its eyes. At the same time, Mark yanked hard on the fishing rod, pulling on the hook, which was still stuck in the evil eel's mouth. The eel reared up in the water, trying to shake off both Frankie and Mark, but it was too late—Frankie had done it again! The zombified eel flopped down onto Mark's boat with a thud. As it fell, its gigantic tail flipped out of the water and struck Frankie like a tennis ball being swatted by a whale. He flew over the waves, heading straight toward a group of rocks farther out to sea.

"Frankie!" I shouted. He was going to land on the rocks. What if he couldn't get back into the water? He'd die! "Quick, Mark, dump the eel and take us out there to get Frankie. You can get us there faster in your motorboat!" I yelled.

Mark looked at the giant eel draped across his boat. "And why would I do that? I've got what I came for," he said as he powered up the engine. "You guys better start rowing *Velma* back. It looks like rain."

He turned *Daphne's Delight* and headed back to shore—the eel lying over the bow of his boat with its head and tail dangling in the water.

"We'll get Frankie ourselves," I said.

Pradeep and I each grabbed an oar and rowed toward where we thought Frankie must have landed, but when we got to the rocks, there was no sign of him. Then we rowed around and tried to spot the green glow of his eyes under the waves.

Drops of rain started to fall on our faces as Sami snuffled, "No swimming now, fishy. Come back!" She shivered in her wet clothes and sneezed.

"We have to get Sami back to the lighthouse," Pradeep said. "She'll get sick if she stays out much longer."

I nodded. We wrapped my jacket around her shoulders and grabbed the oars again.

None of us said anything all the way back to shore.

CHAPTER 10
LIKE A FISH OUTTA WATER

When we got back to the jetty, there was no sign of Mark or *Daphne's Delight* anywhere. We tied up the rowboat and Pradeep gave Sami a piggyback up to the house.

Of course the dads shouted at us when they saw that Sami was wet and sneezing. Until we reminded them that they thought she was still asleep. Then the parent guilt kicked in. Dads get that a lot when they think they are going to be told off by moms for what the kids got up to while they were with the dads.

We told them that we were playing on the shore with Sami when we all got splashed by a really big wave, but that we didn't bring her back right away because she was having so much fun. Amazingly, they seemed to believe us, even though Sami's face looked like she had never had fun in her life.

"Swishy fishy gone," she mumbled as her dad carried her upstairs to dry off and warm up.

"Now let's get some lunch for you two," my dad said to me and Pradeep, wrapping beach towels around our shoulders.

As he put bowls of soup down in front of us, neither of us felt much like eating. I kept picturing Frankie swimming around in the soup bowl.

I even tried a quick brain shake to get rid of the picture in my head, but it didn't make me any less sad. I decided to concentrate on stopping Mark's evil plan instead. It's what Frankie would have wanted us to do.

I gave Pradeep a look that said, "We have to stop Mark from doing whatever he is going to do with the evil eel, whether we have Frankie to help us or not."

Pradeep nodded as he pushed his soup away.

"Can we be excused, please? I don't feel hungry," he said to my dad.

"Of course. You both have a rest and we'll do something nice when Sami gets up from her nap," he said. Then he gave Pradeep his "Chin up, sport, it's not that bad!" look.

Pradeep looked over at me with his "Did your dad just ask me if I wanted yummy Spam for dinner?" look.

I told you they were really similar!

We both left the table and headed upstairs to

change out of our wet clothes and have another look in Mark's room. As our sneakers squelched up the stairs, I thought there had to be a clue to Mark's evil plan somewhere—we just had to find it.

As we finished getting changed, Dad knocked on our bedroom door. He had just come down from Mark's room.

"Have you two seen Mark?" he said. "The lighthouse keeper just mentioned that he saw him take off in the motorboat this morning, but he hasn't come back."

Pradeep and I looked at each other. It hadn't occurred to us that Mark might still be out there with the eel. What if it woke up on the boat and knocked Mark overboard, or if he ran out of fuel or got lost? He might be evil, but I didn't want anything *that* bad to happen to him.

"We saw him go out on the boat when we were playing with Sami," I said.

"He was fishing for the eel," Pradeep added.

Dad got a really worried look on his face.
I know looks, and in one second Dad had
about six different "Worried about this or that
happening to Mark" looks stream across his face.

"I'm sure he's OK," I said.

"I'm sure he is too," Dad replied. Which was a
lie. "I'm sure Mark's fine" was definitely not one
of the looks I saw.

CHAPTER 11
ROWBOAT TO THE RESCUE

"I'm going to go talk to the lighthouse keeper," Dad said. "Pradeep, get your dad and meet me downstairs."

Once the dads and the lighthouse keeper were all in the living room, Pradeep and I lurked in the hall and stared through the glass panels in the closed door. Although we couldn't actually hear what they were saying, Pradeep and I had been practicing lip-reading as an emergency measure in case our secret looks, secret calls, or secret flag signals ever all failed at once. This is what we worked out:

1) Dad had called the local coast guard, but they were already out looking for another missing boat.
2) A coast guard helicopter was being sent from another county, but they said it might take a while.
3) The dads were planning to take the rowboat out before the rain got any worse. They could look for Mark in the coves that the lighthouse keeper knew along the bay. It would take both the dads to row and the lighthouse keeper to show them the way, which would mean leaving us alone to look after Sami.

Pradeep and I stepped forward into the living room.

"You've gotta go look for Mark," we said at the same time. (We still do that sometimes, but we're working on it.)

"Sami will be OK with us," Pradeep added. "We'll give her some soup when she wakes up and keep her warm and safe." He held up his fingers in his Cub Scout salute. "We promise."

For Pradeep that was as good as swearing that he would never have Choc Rice Pops, his favorite food on earth, *ever* again.

The dads both nodded. Maybe this doing-things-at-the-same-time thing was catching.

They headed outside to the rowboat. The rain was getting heavier. I looked at my watch—two p.m. I gave Pradeep a look that said, "They still have loads of time before it gets dark. As long as that fog from last night doesn't come back in again, they'll be fine."

The lighthouse keeper turned to me and said, "If the fog rolls in, we'll just follow the lighthouse beacon back here. That's what it's there for, boy," and he gave me a wink.

Pradeep shot me a look that said, "Our secret looks were just compromised by the old lighthouse keeper. Years of practice down the drain. How did he do that?"

We walked the dads and the lighthouse keeper down to the dock.

"Now, you kids stay outta trouble," the old lighthouse keeper growled. He gave us a sideways look that could have been "And I'll know if you pesky kids have been meddling with my lighthouse too!" Or it could have been "Don't use all the milk as I'll want some for my tea later." It was hard to get the hang of reading his looks through all the wrinkles around his eyes.

Then they all got into *A Vision of Velma* and rowed out into the bay.

As soon as they were gone, Pradeep went to check on Sami, and I headed up to Mark's room to look for more clues.

I walked over to the bed where Mark's suitcase was.

The white lab coat's gone, I thought. The chemistry-set bottles were missing too. And the drawing of the evil eel. Mark must have come back and taken all his stuff to complete his evil plan!

I ran downstairs to tell Pradeep. He had Sami sitting at the kitchen table with a bowl of soup in front of her. He was doing that flying-spoon thing that parents do to get little kids to eat their food. She just shook her head and frowned.

"Pradeep, Mark must have come back here after he caught the eel. He's been in his room. The white lab coat and bottles from the chemistry set and the drawing are all gone!"

Pradeep snuck a mouthful of soup into Sami's mouth as she opened it to yawn.

"But if he came back, then where is the boat? And where is he now?" Pradeep said.

I ran out the door and looked out into the bay. The rowboat was too far away for the dads to hear me shout.

That was when I wished I had learned real semaphore and not the made-up flag signaling that Pradeep and I use. In our version:

Waving a World Cup flag = all's well.
Waving an Olympic flag = someone's coming.
Waving one of the pirate flags that we got

in a party bag one time = danger. Or pirates.

And waving two pirate flags at the same time = dangerous pirates, but we lost one of them, so we're hoping we never *really* meet any dangerous pirates because we won't be able to signal that.

I was about to run back inside to tell Pradeep it was too late to call our dads back when I glanced down. Under the jetty was the motorboat.

CHAPTER 12

THE SECRET EVIL SCIENTIST SCHEME

Daphne's Delight was all tucked up underneath the wooden jetty so you couldn't see it from the lighthouse or from the top of the dock. It had a couple of branches thrown over it to cover it from view. So Mark was definitely back then . . . but what about the evil eel?

I looked over at the lighthouse on the outcrop of rocks jutting into the bay. How could Mark have carried the eel from the boat up the path to the lighthouse or anywhere else? Then I spotted the wheelbarrow. It was at the bottom of the metal fire-escape steps that spiraled around the outside of the lighthouse.

I ran back inside again. Sami turned and smiled at me.

"No more soup," she said. "Ice cream?"

"I think she's feeling better," I said. "Pradeep, come outside. I think I might have figured out where Mark went with the eel. And it's a lot closer than you might think."

We bundled Sami up in a raincoat and hat and went outside. The three of us stood at the bottom of the fire escape and looked up. I showed Pradeep the wheelbarrow and pointed out the boat tucked under the jetty.

"Come on then," Pradeep said, and we all headed up the stairs. The sky had got so dark that the lighthouse beacon had come on above us and was shining out to sea.

At the top of the lighthouse was a balcony with a door leading into the lamp room. The only way to look inside was through a tiny window at the top. Pradeep put Sami on his shoulders so we could find out what was going on.

"Evil eel!" she said. "In kiddie pool."

"Do you see Mark?" I asked.

"No Mark. Naughty eel sleepy," she said.

"We need to get in there and see what he's doing," Pradeep said.

On the count of three, Pradeep, Sami, and I shoved hard on the door. It sprang open easily, sending us flying across the room to land in a tangled heap.

"Morons, I've been expecting you," Mark said with a mocking laugh as he walked over and stroked the head of the sleepy-looking eel.

We jumped up and stood close together in a row. Sami seemed to be pointing at the floor underneath us, where someone had drawn a big chalk line, but we had more important things to worry about.

"We don't know what you're up to, Mark," I said, "but I'm pretty sure it's evil and it involves killing that eel!"

"We can't let you do it," Pradeep added.

"I'm not gonna kill the eel," Mark said with a particularly evil smile, "but I can't have you *meddling kids* trying to stop my *actual* evil plan, so . . ." He paused and pulled on a rope that was hanging next to him. Immediately three life preservers dropped from the ceiling and fell over our heads, trapping us with our arms pinned to our sides like . . . well, like three kids trapped in life preservers!

Mark walked over and wedged the rings more tightly around our arms. "Thanks for standing on the booby-trap line I drew. That made things a lot easier, morons."

We looked down at our feet. If *Scooby-Doo* had taught us anything, it was don't stand in a circle of rope, on anything that could be a trapdoor, or

on a chalk line drawn on the ground. Sami had been trying to warn us and we'd ignored her! Pradeep and I hung our heads in shame.

"Well, as you can see, I'm kinda busy so . . ." Mark started to push us all toward the balcony door.

CHAPTER 13

MWHAHAHAHA HORROR

As Mark shoved us outside into the rain, I looked back at the eel coiled in its shallow rubber kiddie pool. It was still under Frankie's zombie stare! Frankie. He wouldn't have got caught like this. He would have foiled Mark's plan somehow.

"Now you're outta the way, I can get on with my experiment." Mark grinned.

"Experiment?" cried Pradeep, Sami, and I at the same time.

"We thought you were going to kill the evil eel," I said.

"Why would I kill it when I can make it into a zombie eel instead?" Mark said, and laughed his

Evil Scientist laugh. "You have, oh yeah, *had* a pathetic zombie goldfish. But *I'm* gonna have an evil zombie mega-eel, so I can take on anyone that messes with my evil plans. No one's going to give me detention, or ground me, or stop me from taking over the world now!"

"But how are you going to make the evil eel into a zombie like Frankie?" Pradeep asked.

"All I need to do is gunk up the water with my toxic green goo and then add a little spark." Mark grinned.

At that exact moment a flash of lightning and a crash of thunder rocked the lighthouse.

"Sorry, gotta go," Mark said, and slammed and bolted the door, trapping us outside.

"We've got to see what he's doing," I cried. "Pradeep, if you kneel down, I can stand on your life preserver and see in!"

It was a bit wobbly, but I could just about see into the window at the top of the door. Mark walked over to the kiddie pool. He took out a test

tube of green bubbling sludge from his
white lab coat pocket and dumped it in the water
with the eel.

I concentrated on my lip-reading. "Now, I'd
better go get that spark," Mark seemed to say. He
put one end of a long pole into the toxic green
goo with the eel. The other end of the
pole went up through the roof, past the

lighthouse beacon, and into the open air.

I jumped down. Pradeep and Sami looked at me. "Mark's going to use the lightning to shock the eel just like we used a battery on Frankie. The evil eel could be the most evil zombie thing we've ever seen!" my look said. At the same time, I wriggled out of my life preserver. Years of being squeezed through the dog flap at home by Mark meant that I'd had lots of practice wriggling out of things. As soon as I was free, I pulled the rings off Pradeep and Sami, too.

Lightning cracked again all around the lighthouse. Pradeep put his arm around Sami as she pulled her hat down over her ears to drown out the thunder.

I took out the little pirate flag from my pocket and waved it, for all the good it would do. We were in danger, no matter how you looked at it. I wished I had twenty more flags to wave.

Then Pradeep got that look on his face that meant that he had a big idea. "The flag!" he cried. "We can signal for help. Maybe the dads and the lighthouse keeper will see it and come back."

"But how can we signal to them?" I said. "They won't see us waving this flag from here."

Pradeep grinned. "What would Batman do?" he said.

CHAPTER 14

SOZ—
SAVE OUR ZOMBIE!

Pradeep, Sami, and I raced up the next flight of the fire escape to the very top of the lighthouse where the beacon was. We stood on the walkway directly in front of the light. Pradeep and I knelt down and tried to bend ourselves into S shapes, while Sami curled up into an O between us.

We were trying to spell SOS, which Pradeep said means "Save Our Souls." Secretly, I tried to make my S look a bit like a Z so it could stand for *Save Our Zombie!* instead.

Hopefully the dads and the lighthouse keeper would see our signal and come back to shore.

Pradeep said that, technically, we should have

spelled out *Mayday*, but we didn't have enough
people for that.

At that moment, I looked down at the floor
and noticed we were standing on what looked
like a trapdoor. My first thought was, *Have
we learned nothing from the booby-trap thing
before?* But my second thought was, *Hang on!
We can use this to get back into the room below
and stop Mark!*

As quietly as we could, we creaked open the trapdoor and looked down. There was a ladder leading right into the room.

Sami went first, then Pradeep, then me. We were halfway down the ladder when a gust of wind blew the trapdoor shut above our heads.

Slam!

Mark spun around and saw us all hanging on to the ladder. Our cover was totally blown! I tried to go back up through the trapdoor, but it was stuck.

"Morons! How did you . . . ?" He stared at us angrily, then grinned and shook his head. "Never mind, you're too late anyway."

At that instant, a bolt of lightning struck the rod on the roof.

The surge of electricity blew the lighthouse beacon out completely. With all the rain and the fog that had just started to roll in, it was as dark as night outside.

The same flash traveled down the pole to the

eel in his kiddie pool. He flipped just like Frankie had done when we shocked him back to life.

Suddenly the eel reared up, knocking the lightning rod out of the pool and onto the floor. Electric sparks flew from its scales as it writhed. Its eyes tried to focus through a glow of zombie orange.

Mark had done it. He had created an evil zombie mega-eel!

CHAPTER 15

LIGHTHOUSE, FRIGHTHOUSE

Mark took a step toward his giant new zombie pet. "You're mine now and you'll do whatever I say," he commanded. "Now, come here!"

The eel just stared at Mark with his glowing orange eyes.

"I said, come here, moron eel!" Mark shouted.

The eel slid out of the pool toward Mark. Its fins sent tiny electric pulses into the air that made all our hair stand on end. Now Sami, Pradeep, and I actually looked as scared as we felt.

The eel was right in front of Mark now!

"Stop," he said, holding up a hand.

But the eel didn't pay attention. Instead it wound around Mark's legs and coiled around his middle until all you could see was Mark's head sticking out the top of a pile of scales and fins.

"Help!" Mark squelched.

Then I heard a gurgling in the drainpipe against the lighthouse wall, then a rattling of the metal pipe, and then finally a *whoosh* of water as Frankie shot out of the open end of the drain!

"Frankie!" I yelled.

He must have seen our bat signal and swam all the way back from out at sea!

Frankie slid across the floor toward the evil eel, flipped up in front of its face, and spat a mouthful of drain water at him. That got his attention.

The eel unwrapped itself from Mark and tried to swipe its tail at Frankie, but Frankie easily dodged the attack.

Mark crawled out of the way of the eel and over to the ladder.

"Go up!" he yelled.

"The trapdoor won't open!" I yelled back. "We need to come down!"

The only way out was through the door on the other side of the zombie eel.

By now, the two zombie pets were squaring off in the kiddie pool, preparing for a mega-zombie smackdown. (Just so you know, even though it would be an awesome name for a comic book, it's *not* an awesome thing to be stuck in the middle of.)

Frankie's green eyes glowed as he tried to

hypnotize the evil eel. The evil eel's eyes glowed back in a burning, bright-orange zombie stare. Its huge body fizzed and sparked with electricity as it flung itself at Frankie. Frankie leaped in and out of the paddling pool and into the puddles of goopy green water that had splashed onto the floor. Neither of them seemed able to get the upper fin. It was like undersea championship boxing!

Then Sami jumped down from the bottom rung of the ladder, ran past Mark, and jumped between the two angry zombies.

"Stop fighting, naughty fishy things!" she yelled.

"Sami, no!" shouted Pradeep, scrambling down the ladder to get to her.

Both Frankie and the eel were in full zombie-stare mode—and Sami was caught in the zombie-stare crossfire! Suddenly Sami was looking both at the wall of the lighthouse and up the evil eel's left nostril. Her left eye glowed green

and her right
eye was glowing
pale orange.

"Swishy
fishy eel," she
mumbled.

Although he
denied it later,
that's when Mark
totally squealed.

CHAPTER 16

SWISHY FISHY SMACKDOWN

I jumped down from the ladder and only just managed to grab Pradeep before he leaped in and got himself zombified too!

Sami was staring deep into the eyes of the evil eel. Her face suddenly looked very sad. The eel lowered his head and she went over and patted him behind his gills.

Then Sami turned to Frankie. "Don't be mean to Zarky," she said, and wagged her finger at him.

"Zarky?" Pradeep gasped.

"Eel says his name is Zarky," she said to us. "He's sad," she went on. "He tries to play, but people scream and say go away. Some bad people on boats hook Zarky and hurt him. Zarky not evil. He wants friends."

Sami walked over to Frankie. "Say sorry, swishy fishy."

Frankie looked just like I felt when Mom made me apologize to Sara Wartly for splat-bombing her. He looked up at the eel and the green in his eyes faded to a dull glow.

"Now Zarky say sorry to Frankie," Sami said to the eel.

The eel lowered his head and looked at Frankie. His orange eyes dimmed too.

Sami's eyes stopped glowing orange and green, and she giggled.

"I know you're not mean, swishy fishy," she said, picking up Frankie and planting a huge wet kiss on his face. I've never seen a fish look so embarrassed. It was one thing to say sorry, but totally another to get kissed in front of your one-time arch-nemesis.

Pradeep unfolded a sick bag from his pocket, filled it with water from the drain, and held it out for Frankie. He wriggled across and jumped inside.

"This is pathetic," Mark said as he stomped past the eel. "You're not an evil zombie eel at all. You can't even thrash a puny little zombie fish. Next time I'm gonna make a zombie so tough . . ." Mark didn't have a chance to finish his insult. The not-so-evil eel filled its mouth with green gunk from the kiddie pool and squirted it in Mark's face.

"Argh!" Mark yelled. "Stupid eel, stupid fish, stupid vacation!"

"Eel go splat!" Sami said, and giggled. "Now get Zarky home."

Pradeep opened the door to the balcony, and that's when we saw the little rowboat far out in the bay. You could hardly make it out through all the fog and the rain. It looked like a tiny toy boat floating away across a giant pond. Because that's exactly what it was doing. It was heading out to sea.

"They're going the wrong way!" Pradeep cried.

Of course! The beacon had blown when the lightning hit the lighthouse. There was no light to guide them home.

CHAPTER 17

A LIGHT BETWEEN TWO ZOMBIES

"We've got to get the lighthouse beacon back on," I said to Pradeep and Mark, "or they'll never find their way back."

Even Mark looked worried at the idea of the dads getting lost at sea.

We clambered up the fire escape back to the lamp room, leaving Sami with Frankie and Zarky. A huge reflective glass surrounded the giant beacon.

Pradeep tripped the switch on the wall. Nothing happened.

"Swishy fishy!" Sami shouted.

Together we managed to open the trapdoor

again so we could see her at the bottom of the ladder.

Sami was holding Frankie up in his bag. There was a pale-green glow from Frankie's eyes.

"That's it!" I shouted. "We've used Frankie as a night-light before at sleepovers. Maybe his glowing eyes can lead the boat home if the glass reflects the brightness out to sea?"

Pradeep thought for a minute. "His eyes aren't powerful enough," he said. "We'd have to find some way to turbo-boost Frankie's glow."

Then at the same time we said, "Zarky!"

We left Mark in the lamp room, climbed back down the ladder, and explained to Sami, Zarky, and Frankie what we needed them to do. Then Pradeep and I lifted Zarky up the ladder and passed him up to Mark. Sami followed us with Frankie in his sick bag.

Zarky coiled himself in front of the beacon reflector and held Frankie gently between his scaly folds. Frankie's eyes started glowing green.

But Pradeep was right; the glow wasn't strong enough. Then I had an idea.

"Mark, you're a moron," I said.

"What did you just say?" He looked at me and his right hand clenched into a fist.

Frankie's zombie eyes started to glow more brightly.

"Yeah," Pradeep joined in, catching on to what I was doing. "You're a double moron!"

"You losers have a death wish, right?" Mark said, pounding his fist against the palm of his other hand.

Frankie's eyes glowed brighter than ever, but it still wasn't enough to be seen far out at sea. We had to get Zarky to give him the turbo-boost.

"Yeah, anyone who thinks they can trap an eel like Zarky is a moron and a loser," I said.

"Let me get over there. I'm gonna destroy you!" yelled Mark.

I could see Zarky's eyes glowing orange. His coils sparked into life around Frankie.

I took Sami's hand and pulled her away from the giant eel's side.

"Mean Mark, smelly Mark," Sami laughed.

"Stupid little moron!" Mark yelled at Sami. "I'll get you, too. Just you wait!"

That was all they needed.

Zarky's scales sparked like little bonfire-night sparklers and suddenly Frankie's eyes shone like two bulging bright-green lamps. The glass reflected the pulsing glow far out to sea.

CHAPTER 18

BACK TO THE DEEP, GREEN SEA

"Mark, grab those binoculars and see if you can spot the rowboat!" I yelled, trying to distract him from the thumping that was about to come my way.

Scowling and muttering something that sounded like, "I'll get you *all* later," Mark grabbed the binoculars from a hook on the wall and stomped outside.

I held my breath. Then Mark shouted, "I can see them! They're heading back toward the lighthouse."

Frankie and Zarky stayed lit up until the dads were only a few strokes from the jetty.

"Zarky home now?" Sami said quietly. Zarky

uncoiled himself and Frankie jumped back into his sick bag of water.

That's when we heard the rumble of the helicopter outside. Pradeep and I helped Zarky to the balcony.

"Look, it's the coast guard!" I shouted to Pradeep above the noise of the whirring blades as the helicopter hovered over the jetty.

The dads were just tying the boat up. They waved up to the helicopter pilots, who gave them a thumbs-up sign.

"We'd better get Zarky out of here before the coast guard spots us!" Pradeep yelled.

"I don't know how we're going to get him down!" I shouted back.

"I don't think we're going to need to!" Pradeep bellowed, pointing at the water below.

Zarky gently lifted his tail to pat Sami on the head. Then he turned and nodded to Frankie, and with one powerful thrust he leaped over the balcony railing and into the sea. Sparks flashed

off his scales as he
hit the water.

"Sparky Zarky!"
Sami said, and
clapped her hands.

The helicopter
flew up from
the jetty and
circled above the
lighthouse.

A booming voice
came out of the loudspeaker on the helicopter.
"Are you kids OK? We just saw . . . Well, we're not
sure what we just saw," it said.

We gave the pilots a thumbs-up too.

"Is the missing boy still at sea?" the pilots asked.

Pradeep and I shouted together, "No, that's
him!" and pointed to Mark, who looked even
grumpier than before.

They waved and circled once more before
heading off down the coast.

Mark complained all the way down the stairs, but every time he stopped walking, Frankie jumped in the sick bag and splashed water at him until he carried on.

At the front door of the lighthouse we met our dads and the lighthouse keeper.

"We found Mark," I said, holding the sick bag with Frankie in it behind my back. "He was upstairs in the lamp room."

"We thought you were out in the boat! You can't just disappear like that! You are in big trouble!" Dad yelled at Mark. Then his eyes softened. "But I'm glad you're OK, Son."

He gave Mark a hug.

Mark did not look pleased.

"I suppose you made a mess of my shipshape lighthouse as well, did ya?" the lighthouse keeper grumbled.

"Um," Mark said, "it was the morons' fault, they—"

The lighthouse keeper interrupted him. "Then

you can spend tomorrow mopping and cleaning it up till it shines like the scales of an eel," he said.

Pradeep's dad turned to Sami. "And how are you, little precious?"

"Daddy, swishy fishy came back and we climbed high and eel went buzzzzzzzz, and then fishy and eel go zap, zap, and then shiny, shiny light and Zarky go splash and you come home." She took a deep breath and gave her dad a huge hug.

Pradeep's dad gave Pradeep a look that said, "Huh?"

We all went inside, and since nobody had caught any fish, we ordered pizza for dinner. I made sure to get one with green peppers and spinach for Frankie. No mould or green cupcake crumbs for him tonight. We had a big day out in the boat to look forward to, while the lighthouse keeper made Mark clean up.

CHAPTER 19

THE MYSTERY OF EEL BAY

The next day was bright and sunny. By the time we got up and out, there were already lots of boats on the water, and cars were pulling into the lighthouse drive to ask the lighthouse keeper if he had any rooms to rent.

"We heard there was a giant electric eel in these waters," one lady said.

"A coast guard helicopter filmed it leaping off the lighthouse and sparking all the way down to the water! It was all over the TV this morning," another man with a fancy camera said.

As we rowed away in *A Vision of Velma*, the lighthouse keeper shot me a look from the jetty that said, "Thanks," and he smiled.

I looked over at Pradeep to see whether he had seen the lighthouse keeper's look, and then we both shot him back a look that said, "How do you know our looks?"

His answer look said, "Do you young whipper-snappers think I was never ten years old? I invented secret looks before you were even born!"

With that he tipped his flat cap to us and went off to shout at Mark to mop up a spot he had missed on the stairs.

When we looked back toward the jetty, he was waving a small World Cup flag.

"Darn, he invented that, too!" Pradeep and I both looked at each other as the dads rowed.

When we reached the middle of the bay, we got out our cameras, trying to catch a glimpse of the amazing giant electric eel.

Dad reached down for the cooler at my feet. "Good idea to bring some drinks, Tom," he said.

"With all this rowing, I've worked up quite a thirst." I quickly shot Pradeep a look that said, "SOS!"

"Wow, look over there!" Pradeep yelled. "I think I see the eel."

Everyone turned to look the other way.

I quickly reached into the cooler and scooped Frankie out. As I cupped him in my hands I whispered, "Time for a swim, Frankie, but not for so long this time, OK?"

He flipped into the water with a splash.

"Swishy fishy go swimming!" Sami squealed.

"I do hope we get to see the eel before it's time to go back," said Pradeep's dad.

As if on cue, Zarky flew into the air in front of our boat, electric sparks flying off his fins as he jumped.

Cameras clicked and tourists gasped. Zarky turned to us and gave us a little eel smile. I think he was enjoying all the attention. He came down with a mighty splash just by some boats. But this

time no one screamed or called him evil. Instead they all clapped.

"Oh, doesn't he look beautiful when he sparkles against the water?" one tourist said as she snapped a close-up.

With all the attention on Zarky, no one seemed to notice a little gold fleck in the water swimming beside him. I zoomed in with my camera to get a closer look. Frankie was jumping through the waves in time with Zarky, followed by a whole school of new fishy friends.

"You know what, Pradeep?" I grinned. "I kinda like being a meddling kid on a mystery adventure, as long as we've got our zombie goldfish along for the ride."

TO BE A ZOMBIE
OR NOT TO BE A
ZOMBIE . . . THAT
IS THE QUESTION

CHAPTER 1
RUN, ZOMBIE, RUN

Pradeep and I ran down the road toward the school gates.

"Come on, we're gonna be late," Pradeep shouted over his shoulder. He was way ahead of me. Not because he's a faster runner, but because:

a) Frankie, my pet zombie goldfish, was in a plastic bag in my backpack and the water kept sloshing from side to side as I ran, which kinda threw my balance off.

b) I was carrying a big wooden stick under each arm.

c) I was running toward school an hour earlier than I actually had to be there and every cell in my body was telling me that this was just wrong!

NOOOOO!!!

Frankie was pretty shaken up from all this running and that didn't make him happy. I don't know if any of you have dealt with a pet zombie goldfish that's been brought back to life by battery after he'd been fatally gunked with toxic stuff—but they're not exactly chilled-out pets.

We raced through the gates, up the front

steps, and down the corridor into the main hall. By the time we arrived at the auditions for the school play, Pradeep and I were panting. And we weren't even the first ones to get there! There was already a long line that snaked out of the side door and down past the dressing rooms.

"I thought we'd be first here," Pradeep said, looking around.

"At least there's time for extra breakfast," I said, unpacking all the snacks we'd brought.

"You're right," Pradeep said, digging Frankie out of the bag too. "We're gonna need it."

Frankie glared at me and Pradeep.

"Sorry, Frankie," I whispered. "We were running late."

Now, Pradeep eats when he's nervous and I eat when I'm bored, so between us we hoovered up our snack rations pretty fast.

Two granola bars, three apples, and several of Pradeep's mom's samosas later, we were *still*

waiting, along with Kevin Bradley (the junior choir champion) outside the hall doors.

Suddenly I noticed that Kevin was mumbling "Swishy little fishy . . ." and picking out green M&M's from his lunch box. Frankie must have rolled his bag over there and hypnotized Kevin in search of a snack! (Zombie goldfish have a thing about anything green—especially food!)

"I guess Frankie needed a second breakfast too," I sighed.

After we'd convinced Frankie to un-hypnotize Kevin (but only after making him forget he ever saw a zombie goldfish with hypnotic powers), we gave Frankie some mouldy bits of old samosa that we'd saved for him, then zipped him up tight in the backpack. We couldn't risk him being spotted again.

"I knew you shouldn't have brought Frankie," Pradeep said as he paced up and down the corridor after Kevin had gone in to do his audition.

"I had to," I said back. "The first rehearsal is right after school. I couldn't risk Mark being home alone with Frankie until we got back." Frankie still holds a pretty big grudge against Mark, my Evil Scientist big brother, for trying to murder him with toxic gunk as part of one of his evil experiments.

"Oh, OK." Pradeep nodded. "But don't you mean *if* we get cast in the show?"

"She'd be crazy not to pick us," I said. "Where else is she gonna find better stick-fighting, arrow-shooting, rope-swinging Merry Men in this school?"

Pradeep smiled. He knew it was true. We had practiced jumping off things and onto things, swinging from things, fighting with things, shooting at things, and generally being the best Merry Men any Robin Hood could ever want. This year the play was going to be epic.

I peeked through the door into the hall.

Kevin was onstage doing his song. It would be our turn next. "Was it this long a wait at the auditions last year, Pradeep?" I asked.

"No, but it wasn't really an audition. They just said yes to everyone that showed up," he said. "This new drama teacher said she's holding proper auditions this year."

I hadn't done the school play in a while. Not since kindergarten when we did the Nativity  story and I tried to add a little action. The teacher didn't think a ninja donkey would have been at the manger. I disagreed.

After I started kickboxing with

a couple of Wise Men, the teacher said maybe I should stick to backstage stuff in the future. And that's what I'd done. But this year was the first time they'd picked a real action play, and it was a musical, too, so I told Pradeep I'd come with him to try out.

He had been in loads of the plays, but he still got nervous.

"You'll be fine, Pradeep," I said as he took off his glasses to clean them for the twenty-third time that hour. "You always get a part," I added.

"Yeah, but always as the same thing," he moaned.

"That's not true. What were you again in that cowboy musical in first grade?"

"A cactus," he said.

"Oh yeah, and in *Aladdin* the next year?"

"A palm tree," he answered.

"Um, OK," I said, biting my lip. "But last year in that eco-musical thing you had a really good part, didn't you?"

"I was a ginkgo," he sighed.

"A really cool lizard kind of thing, right?" I checked.

"No, that's a gecko," he groaned. "A ginkgo is a tree!" Pradeep looked down at his feet. "I don't care if I get to be a Merry Man or a guard or whatever this time. I just don't want to be a plant again."

That was it! We had to get the parts of Merry Men now to prove that I could do an action part (better than the ninja donkey) and that Pradeep could do more than play a tree.

Kevin *finally* came out and it was our turn. As I double-checked that Frankie was still safe in the backpack, I started thinking about the kindergarten Nativity play again. I think I was getting myself back in the ninja zone for the audition. I slipped the backpack over my shoulder as we walked into the school hall.

"Pradeep, what were you in the kindergarten Nativity play?" I wondered.

"I guess it wasn't very memorable." He
paused. "I was the Christmas tree."

CHAPTER 2

THE PLAY'S THE THING

Pradeep and I walked into the hall, where the first thing we saw was Mrs. Flushcowski, the new drama teacher. Can I just say, if you have a name with a toilet sound *and* a farm animal in it, you should just give up and not become a teacher. There's just no challenge in making up a teacher nickname when you start with that.

"Darlings," she said. She called everybody "darling." She leaned back in her director's chair, holding a cup of tea. "Impress me!"

I carefully placed the backpack in the front row, away from Mrs. Flushcowski, and unzipped it a little so Frankie could see us on the stage. I think he deserved to see our big moment. We got out our wooden sticks and started play-fighting with them. We really showed off our jumping and hitting-things skills. Just as we were about to show off our swinging-on-things skills, she stopped us.

"Darlings, you don't have a song? Or a piece prepared?"

"This is our piece," I said. "We want to be Merry Men. So we wanted to show we could pretend fight."

"I need to see that you can *ACT*," she said, but said the word *ACT* in a really weird way like she was saying something important; like the name of the World Computer Games Champion or something. "When I was 'Woman in Elevator' on *The Days of Our Time*, the director said that my every thought was written on my face. Like that. I need to see true *ACTING*."

I whispered to Pradeep, "She wants us to act

merry, I guess. You know, *Merry* Men would be merry as they fight."

"How do you do that?" he asked.

"Follow my lead," I whispered.

I grabbed the big stick and started to fight with Pradeep again.

"Ho, ho, ho," I said. "I got you!"

"Huh?"

"Ho, ho, ho," I said again louder, and then whispered, "I'm being merry!"

"Oh, yeah! Ho, ho, ho," Pradeep said and banged his stick against mine.

"Darlings, darlings, *DARLINGS!*" Mrs. Flushcowski had to shout three times to be heard over the sound of the sticks crashing together and the Santa laughing. "That is *enough.*"

"Do we get the parts, Mrs. Flushcowski?" I asked.

"Do you have nothing prepared that you can recite or sing?" she asked.

Unfortunately, the only song that came into my mind was the Squeaky Clean Toilets advert jingle. I took a deep breath and sang out: *"Ah, so clean and fresh . . . think your guests . . . with Squeaky Clean Toilets."*

"Um, thank you, Tom," Mrs. Flushcowski said, but her look either said, "I have no idea why this young man is here" or "I am in awe at this young man's talent." The two looks are pretty close.

Then Pradeep opened his mouth and started saying a poem.

"I think that I shall never see,
A poem lovely as a tree,
A tree that looks at God all day,
And lifts its leafy arms to pray. . . ."

And he went on.

By the time he finished, I was standing there with my mouth gaping open, Frankie was looking out from his bag with *his* mouth gaping open and Mrs. Flushcowski was actually crying. She dug in her handbag for tissues and dabbed at her face. Then she ran onstage and hugged Pradeep.

I bet that was *not* the reaction he was going for with that poem.

"I had to memorize it last year when I played the ginkgo. It just stuck in my head," he mumbled from somewhere underneath Mrs. Flushcowski.

Mrs. Flushcowski pulled back and stood in front of Pradeep. "You moved me, *darling*," she said.

"I'm sorry," said Pradeep. "You didn't have to get up."

"No, you have *moved* me"—she pointed to her heart—"in here." Then she hugged him again.

When she had pulled herself together, after she had used up about a pack of tissues re-dabbing her eyes, she said, "Thank you. I'll post the cast list later today." And she winked at Pradeep. Then she looked at me and said, "*ACTING*," in that same weird way again, and shook her head. Frankie thrashed in his bag so hard that it made the backpack fall off the seat. Somehow I didn't think my fish was loving Mrs. Flushcowski right now. I jumped down into the front row and grabbed the bag, zipping it up in one swoop. "OK, right, *ACTING*, sure thing," I mumbled as we rushed out of the room.

That afternoon when Pradeep and I went to check the cast list, we saw:

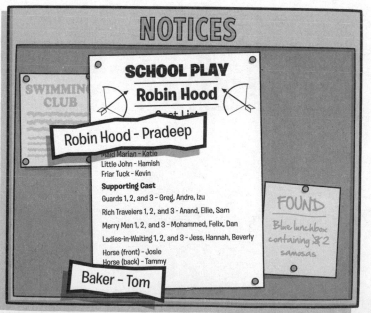

NOTICES

SWIMMING CLUB

SCHOOL PLAY
Robin Hood
Cast List

Robin Hood - Pradeep

Maid Marian - Katie
Little John - Hamish
Friar Tuck - Kevin
Supporting Cast
Guards 1, 2, and 3 - Greg, Andre, Izu
Rich Travelers 1, 2, and 3 - Anand, Ellie, Sam
Merry Men 1, 2, and 3 - Mohammed, Felix, Dan
Ladies-in-Waiting 1, 2, and 3 - Jess, Hannah, Beverly
Horse (front) - Josie
Horse (back) - Tammy

Baker - Tom

FOUND
Blue lunchbox containing £2 samosas

I didn't even know there was a baker in *Robin Hood*. I've read the book and seen at least two movie versions *and* a cartoon of it, and none of those had a baker. I turned around to say that to Pradeep, but he was surrounded by other kids from the cast, getting high fives from the Merry Men. I went to do our special celebration high five with Pradeep anyway, because at least he got a good part, but he didn't even turn around (which made me look like I was fist-bumping with some invisible kid).

Of course I didn't realize it then, but that is exactly when it happened. At 3.03 p.m. on Tuesday afternoon, Pradeep started to change.

CHAPTER 3

NO SMALL PARTS, ONLY SMALL GOLDFISH

I followed Pradeep and the rest of the cast to the first rehearsal and we all lined up and got our scripts. Frankie was still in my backpack. He'd been pretty good today, apart from that hypno-incident with Kevin this morning. I just had to get through the hour of rehearsal without Frankie zombifying anyone and we'd be fine.

Pradeep sat on a chair with the other "main cast" kids, and I sat on the floor with the rest of the "supporting cast." You know, Rich Travelers One, Two, and Three. Guards One, Two, and Three. Ladies-in-Waiting One, Two, and Three, and Merry Men One, Two, and Three. I was the

only supporting-cast person without a number.

But they still *all* had more lines than me.

I had one line: "Robin, there is no bread."

Pradeep had pages of stuff to learn. Loads of lines, a song with Maid Marian, and a big escape number with the Merry Men. *And* he had loads of fight scenes. The baker didn't even get to throw bread rolls at anyone. Pradeep got to fire arrows and fight with sticks and pretend to swing across the stage (which he couldn't do for real in the play for insurance reasons after the school's Peter Pan ended up in the hospital one year with a flying-related injury).

SIGH!

I went up to Pradeep at the end of rehearsal.

"Hey, Pradeep, do you want to come back to my place and start to build the 'Supremely Secret Message Chute' between our bedrooms? I've got the notebook with the drawings and . . ."

But Pradeep hardly looked up. "I can't today. We've got an extra rehearsal for the leads. I don't really have time for that kind of thing anymore." He grabbed his stuff and headed out with the rest of the main cast kids.

I slung the backpack with Frankie in it over my shoulder and shuffled toward the doors. "Come on, Frankie, let's go," I said. "At least you've got time for *that kind of thing*." As I trudged down the front steps of school, Mark swooshed past me on his skateboard, his white Evil Scientist lab coat flapping behind him. I jumped back just in time to avoid being run over.

"Ha, loser," Mark mumbled as he skidded to a stop. "Talking to yourself! Pathetic."

Frankie thrashed hard in the backpack,

trying to fling himself at Mark. "Wait! Were you talking to the moron fish in your backpack? That's even worse! So, so sad."

"Leave us alone, Mark!" I yelled. I unzipped Frankie from the backpack and he glared at Mark.

"Looks like your moron friend Pradeep has got a life and dumped you." Mark smirked. "Who can blame him? I mean, *everyone* has a bigger part in that play than you. They even asked a couple of the eighth graders to do the lights and stuff. Didn't trust you morons not to mess it up for Mrs. Flushcowski's special guest."

"What special guest?" I asked, trying to stop Frankie from hurling himself at Mark.

"I guess they didn't think you were important enough to tell." Mark jumped back on his skateboard and sped off down the road.

I looked at Frankie. "Mark's not right, you know," I said, this time looking around to see if anyone could see me talking to my backpack. "Pradeep hasn't stopped being my friend. You'll see. It'll be better tomorrow."

But the next day, and every day after that, it got worse. Pradeep had dance practice, then fight practice, then song practice . . . or maybe "make your best friend feel like a total waste of space" practice? OK, so that last one wasn't real, but Pradeep wouldn't have needed any help doing that anyway. He was getting it just fine.

There was *always* some kind of practice or rehearsal with just the main cast kids. Especially with the girl playing Maid Marian, Katie Plefka. She was always hanging on to Pradeep like a picture hangs on a wall or like a monkey hangs on a tree or like an annoying girl hangs on your best friend.

The following Monday, having not seen Pradeep all weekend, I went over to him as he was getting his coat. Frankie had come along with me in my backpack for moral support. I thought maybe I could get him to zombify Katie into not being so clingy with Pradeep, or maybe even zombify Pradeep to go back to being normal, but Frankie wasn't in a zombifying mood.

"Hey, Pradeep, are you coming over tonight for *MONDAY ZOMBIE GAMES MADNESS*?" I did it in the movie-announcer voice that Pradeep and I always use when we say "Monday Zombie Games Madness." It just doesn't sound right if you say it in a normal voice.

Katie Plefka started giggling. "What is that?"

"Pradeep and I do it every Monday night." I smiled at Pradeep. "It's zombie computer games and it's . . . *MADNESS*!" I said *madness* again in the announcer voice, expecting Pradeep to join in like he always did. But he didn't. He just looked at me funny, then turned to Katie and said, "It's not like it's every Monday night or anything." He picked up his coat from the chair.

"Yeah, it is," I said.

"No, it's not, Tom. Anyway, I'm heading back with some of the other *actors* later. We're gonna run through the big end scene again." (He had started saying *actors* in the same way Mrs. Flushcowski did.)

"But . . . you can't miss Monday Zombie Games Madness," I said, not bothering with the movie-announcer voice this time. "You didn't even miss it when you had chicken pox and you had to play by walkie-talkie from your room."

Katie giggled again.

"Well, I'm missing it today," Pradeep said, shoving his arm into his coat sleeve.

"Just so you can rehearse for a stupid play!" I shouted.

Other kids were watching us now and Frankie started thrashing around in my backpack too. I don't think he liked us shouting at each other.

"It's not stupid. You're stupid!" Pradeep yelled back.

"You're super-stupid!" I shouted back.

"And you're stupid to the power of stupid zillion!" Pradeep shouted again. That was the first thing he'd said to me in days that sounded like the real Pradeep. My friend Pradeep, not the "Oh, I'm so important, I'm Robin Hood, I'm an ACTOR" Pradeep that I was fighting with.

On my walk home, I thought of twenty funny put-downs that I could have come back with.

All I'd thought to say at the time was, "Fine, I'll have MONDAY ZOMBIE GAMES MADNESS on my own." And I did the movie-announcer voice again too, just to bug him. "It'll be way better anyway."

But it wasn't.

After that I ended up bringing Frankie to all the rehearsals with me. He was good company. I think even the numbered-part kids thought that it was below them to hang out with me, and Pradeep hadn't talked to me since the day we had the fight. I taught Frankie some of the games that Pradeep and I used to play when we got bored. He couldn't do Rock, Paper, Scissors, but he could do Splat, Splosh, Grrr, which are the three sounds that Frankie can make. A Splat beats a Splosh, but gets trumped by a Grrr. Grrr wins against Splat but loses to Splosh, and a Splosh gets trounced by Splat but smacks down a Grrr. He got pretty good at it too, but then again, we had a lot of time to practice.

When I had to be onstage, he just swam around in his bag, hidden inside my backpack. He thrashed about a bit when Mrs. Flushcowski spoke, especially if she was shouting at someone. But when Katie Plefka sang her Maid Marian solo, he looked as if he was actually dancing with joy in the water. Most of the time she was really giggly and kinda annoying, but when she sang, I had to admit, it was OK. It really seemed to chill Frankie out, and he is very critical when it comes to singing. She did sing

"Greensleeves" though, so I guess that is a zombie goldfish– friendly song (being about green sleeves and all).

The only chance I had to talk to Pradeep was when Mrs. Flushcowski made me help him learn his lines.

"Tom, *darling*," she said, "can you take a moment and run lines with Pradeep? He has ever so many to get under his belt before tomorrow."

I mumbled under my breath, "He's not even wearing a belt!"

"What, *darling*?" she asked.

"Nothing," I moaned. I walked over to Mrs. Flushcowski, carrying Frankie in the backpack.

I guess I hadn't zipped it all the way up because she said, "*Darling*, why do you have a goldfish in a plastic bag in rehearsal?"

Pradeep grabbed the backpack. "He's mine,

Mrs. Flushcowski. He's kind of a good-luck charm for the show."

She smiled at Pradeep. "You know, I heard that Laurence Olivier was very taken with goldfish as well."

I stomped over to a couple of chairs with Pradeep. As soon as we sat down, I grabbed the backpack back off him. "You might have everyone else in this school on your side, but you don't have Frankie!" I said. Frankie's eyes darted back and forth between Pradeep and me. I couldn't look at him so I zipped up the bag.

"Let's just get on with this," Pradeep said, looking at his script. It was covered in green highlighter pen.

My script had my one line circled in pencil.

"If you read from page twenty-seven, 'I'll never surrender . . .'" Pradeep said. "You can test me on that bit."

Normally, I would have made a joke with Pradeep about never surrendering to zombies or

Evil Scientist brothers, but no jokes came.

We just ran the lines.

Finally it was the day of the play. We were having the dress rehearsal in the afternoon and the performance that night. Mrs. Kumar, Pradeep's mom, had come in to help out with costumes. My costume was on the list as "general peasant's clothes," which meant I got to wear whatever leftover trousers and shirts were in the back of the costume cupboard, rolled in dirt, plus an oversize baker's hat. I didn't even get to do the rolling in dirt bit with the clothes on. They did that before. Total con!

Mrs. Kumar was straightening Pradeep's tunic and cape. "I'm done, Mom. They need me onstage now. I am Robin Hood, after all—you know, the star of the show?" Pradeep squirmed away from his mom's fussing.

"Oh, someone is getting a big head for a little man," Mrs. Kumar said.

She hiked up his tights in a way that just couldn't be comfortable, handed him his hat, and said, "*Now* you are done. You can go."

CHAPTER 4

DRESS-REHEARSAL DRAMA

Once we were all made-up and in our costumes, we had to wait on the stage for our pep talk with Mrs. Flushcowski. Pradeep somehow managed to look cool in his green tunic and hat with a feather in it. OK, so he had to wear tights, but still.

Mrs. Kumar beamed up at us from the front row. Sami, Pradeep's three-year-old sister, was there too. She was watching Frankie for me while we rehearsed, playing with him at the back of the hall.

We all sat on the stage in our costumes and waited. Then Mrs. Flushcowski entered the

room. And she made "an entrance," as she
was always telling us kids to do. She flounced
in and stood in front of us all, pacing up and
down the stage for *ages* before she said anything.
Then she took a deep breath and spoke very
seriously.

"I have a very important announcement,"
she said. "We are having a special visitor attend
tonight's performance."

Then she did one of her really long pauses
again. This must have been the person Mark was
talking about.

"I worked with him when I appeared as 'Nurse
in Hallway' on *Emergency Hospital,* and he's
always remembered me. He is in town and has
said he will come to see the rising talent that this
school has to offer. He is none other than the
acclaimed judge of *Talent or No Talent*—Solomon
Caldwell!"

The whole cast gasped. I didn't see what the
big deal was. What was Solomon Caldwell going

to say to me—"Wow, that walking baker's hat's got talent?" I didn't think so.

"Everything must be *PERFECT* for tonight. Do you understand?" Mrs. Flushcowski looked at me in particular. "Oh yes, one more thing— this will be the first time that the eighth-grade boys will be helping us as stage crew. I've asked them to come in to make sure the special effects and lighting will be just right. Remember that they are doing this to be helpful, so please, be helpful to them." A group of eighth-graders

dressed in black T-shirts stepped out from backstage.

"Hello," Mark said, striding across the stage with a smoke machine. He put it in its position offstage right. "That's right, we're gonna be *really* helpful." He grinned.

Oh no! Of all the boys she could get, why did it have to be my Evil Scientist big brother? He was dressed in a black T-shirt and jeans. No evil scientist lab coat today. Maybe that was a sign that he wasn't going to be evil. Maybe he really was just going to work on the show and that was it.

Mark walked over to me and spoke in a low whisper: "They said I had to take off my white lab coat. Gotta be all in black so no one can see me in the dark. It gets pretty dark backstage, moron." Then he did his Evil Scientist laugh, "Mwhahahaha," and smiled.

Mrs. Flushcowski turned around, "Very impressive evil laugh, young man. I had to do a laugh like that when I played 'Female Head in Jar' in the Evil Scientist classic *Help! I've Created a Monster*. It's not as good as mine, but it's good," she added.

As soon as she turned to go Mark hissed, "Hey, moron, break a leg! That's what they say in the theater, right?" and he got that creepy smile again.

This was a Code Orange situation at least. I turned to Pradeep to shoot him a look that said, "We're in big trouble because Mark is here and definitely out to get us." But for the first time since we came up with our code of looks, Pradeep was not looking back at me.

It was no good. Pradeep was too wrapped up in the show to notice that we were in danger. It was all up to me now. I was just about to sneak offstage to see what Mark was up to when Mrs. Flushcowski called out, "Places!"

I'd learned that when she says that she means it's time to get to where you are meant to be at the start of the show. It was theater code, I guessed.

As we were rushing to our places, I peeked under the closing curtain and saw Mrs. Kumar motion for Sami to come and sit next to her in the front row. Sami walked slowly over to the seat, carrying my backpack with Frankie in it. Then I saw it. She was looking at the stage and up her mom's left nostril.

Sami had the Frankie zombie goldfish stare!

CHAPTER 5
SWISHY FISHY FACE

"Ready?" Mrs. Flushcowski called out from her director's chair right in front of the stage. She placed her script and a cup of tea on the table in front of her. "Curtain up . . . now!" she declared.

The lights went down and the curtain rose. In the darkness I could see two little green glowing points coming from the unzipped backpack on Sami's lap. Frankie must have heard Mark's voice! I could imagine him going all zombie thrash fish inside the bag, his eyes blazing a brilliant revenge green.

Without her mom noticing, Sami quietly got

up and moved to the side of the stage. She lifted up the backpack and I could see Frankie roll his plastic bag out and toward stage left. Then the green glow disappeared.

"Thank goodness someone put out those green lights. Action!" Mrs. Flushcowski called.

So now the dress rehearsal was starting, Mark was in charge of the smoke machine offstage right and Frankie was rolling around in his bag offstage left! I needed to stop the two of them from bumping into each other behind the scenes and bumping each other off (well, off the stage at least!).

From my starting place in the crowd of supporting cast members, I waved at Pradeep to try to tell him what was going on, but he just looked ahead, concentrating on his *ACTING*. I *had* to get his attention somehow.

In the first scene he had to rob some rich travelers and then give the money to the poor.

As the travelers rode onto the stage, I tried our "Look at me! There is something important I need to tell you!" yawn, but got nothing.

Then, when Pradeep was jumping out at the travelers to rob them I tried our "There's danger here!" pretend coughing fit. Still, nothing.

If I thought that anyone else would believe that my Evil Scientist big brother was about to undertake some kind of evil plot, then I would have yelled it from center stage. But I only knew one person who would understand what was happening, and that was the one person who wasn't talking to me.

As a last resort, I tried our "random owl calls in a place where there wouldn't be owls to show that something's wrong" noise, but unfortunately

I did it right before Pradeep's line about sending a bird with a message to Maid Marian.

Mrs. Flushcowski shouted, "Brilliant bird noise. That's your talent, Tom. Well done!"

Nothing was working!

That was when I saw it. Mark had climbed up onto the metal rigging above the stage where the curtains were hung. He was hooking what looked like a small garbage bag to a pole right

next to the rope that Pradeep was meant to swing from in the next scene. The weird thing was, the bag was wriggling.

Whatever Mark was doing, it had evil plan written all over it.

Then I saw Sami on the opposite side of the stage, just out of sight of Mrs. Flushcowski. She was waving and trying to get Pradeep's attention too, but he was turned out to the audience, saying his big speech about how he wouldn't rest until he had stopped the Sheriff of Nottingham and his evil ways. I couldn't help thinking that some real-life evil ways needed sorting out first!

I owl-hooted to get Sami's attention.

"No more birds in this scene, Tom, thank you, *darling*," Mrs. Flushcowski bellowed.

But it had worked. Sami looked over at me. She didn't look zombified anymore. But she did look very worried.

I shot her a look to ask what was wrong. Now this was risky, as I had never tried communicating in looks with Sami before, and I had no idea if it would work.

She looked scared. Then she looked up at the bag Mark had hung above the stage.

After that she did a pretty good impression

of a goldfish face, looked up at the bag again, did a silent "Mwhahahaha" Evil Scientist laugh, and then looked over at Pradeep.

Sami was telling me that Frankie was in the bag above the stage. Mark had put him there as part of his evil plan, and Pradeep was in danger. You could tell Sami was Pradeep's sister. He had taught her well.

As I looked up at the bag, I could see the faint glimmer of two tiny green dots shining through the dark plastic.

I had to do something to save Frankie and warn Pradeep. But what?

CHAPTER 6

PRE-PLAY PANDEMONIUM

Finally the lights and the curtain went down and everyone got ready for the next scene, which opened with Pradeep hanging on to the rope above the stage, pretending to swing while the scenery moved past him. This was apparently safer than having him swing across the stage, but with Mark's evil plan in action, nothing was safe.

My job was to carry a tree past Pradeep as he hung there. Lady-in-Waiting Number Three had a cardboard horse, Guard Number Three had a small cottage, and Merry Man Number Two had another tree.

All the other supporting cast kids had big pieces of cardboard offstage that they were fanning up and down to make lots of wind as Pradeep "whooshed" along.

Kids were running all over the place, trying to get to their places. It was so dark, you could hardly see a thing.

I ran over to Pradeep. "You can't swing on the rope. It might be rigged!"

"Of course it's rigged. That's the safety thing. I don't swing on it, remember. It's fine, Tom," he whispered.

"No, it's a trick—" I started to say, but he cut me off.

"Not now. I gotta do the scene."

"But Frankie . . ." I started to say, but the curtain was already rising. As the lights came up, Pradeep grabbed ahold of the rope.

There was no time for me to try to climb up and stop Mark. Besides, Pradeep *would* listen to me about something this important, right?

150

As I ran behind Pradeep with my cardboard tree, I hissed, "Let go of the rope!"

Then Lady-in-Waiting Three ran by carrying her cardboard horse.

I looked up and could see Mark trying to hold on to the black bag, but at the same time fiddling with the rope that Pradeep was hanging from.

I raced around the back of the stage while Merry Man Two was running past with the other tree, and got to Guard Three just in time to snatch the cardboard cottage from him and dash past Pradeep again, "I'm serious, Pradeep. You have to let go!"

"Tom, you're ruining this for me. Leave me alone!"

Just as he said it, the rope dropped from the rigging and Pradeep fell onto the stage. At the same time, the black bag slipped out of Mark's hands. It was too late! I could see Frankie's eyes glowing inside the dark bag as it tumbled toward the hard stage. Pradeep looked up and saw the green glow too. . . .

"Frankie?" he yelled. He held out his green cape to try to catch the bag as it fell, but the bag bounced off and into the cardboard cutout of the cottage that I was carrying. I was knocked backward, falling into the tree and the horse and the kids that were holding them. All the cardboard scenery toppled over like a row of dominoes. Someone fell into the curtains and started to pull them down. As the rest of the cast ducked for cover, the bag with Frankie in it once again hurtled toward the floor. . . .

Leaping forward, Pradeep stretched out his cape again to try to break Frankie's fall, but the green fabric acted like a trampoline and bounced the bag straight at Mrs. Flushcowski.

There was nothing we could do!

It splatted on the table right in front of her, soaking her with water. Everyone in the hall went quiet for what was probably a second but

seemed like hours. I tried to see Frankie, but I couldn't spot him from the stage.

Mrs. Flushcowski turned bright red and shouted, "Mr. Kumar! I suppose you think that's funny?"

I think at first when Mrs. Flushcowski said "Mr. Kumar," Pradeep was genuinely looking around for his dad, but she was just doing that "I'm being a very serious teacher now" thing where they call you by your last name.

"Oh, me? Right. I don't think it's funny, well, not much, I mean . . ." Pradeep said, looking confused. "I don't know what happened!"

"I'll tell you what happened, Mr. Kumar: You have ruined my dress rehearsal and . . ." She did another of her really long, dramatic pauses as she took a deep breath and picked up her cup of tea from the table in front of her. "You have lost yourself the role of Robin Hood!"

There was a gasp from the other kids.

"But—" Pradeep started to say.

"Never, in all my years in theater, has one

of my cast members, especially not the leading *ACTOR*, thrown a water bomb at me!"

Suddenly, at the same time, Pradeep and I spotted Frankie.

"You may think a prank like that is funny, young man," she went on, lifting her tea to her lips.

"Mrs. Flushcowski . . ." Pradeep tried to interrupt her again.

"But it will not be tolerated at this sch—" she started to say and then spluttered out her tea with a shriek.

Frankie leaped out of her mouth and back into the teacup!

Mrs. Flushcowski fell back into her chair and fainted.

CHAPTER 7

SECOND IN THE SPOTLIGHT

Pradeep and I both raced off the stage. Mrs. Kumar ran over from her seat and Sami appeared from the side of the stage, carrying her little lidded drinking cup filled with water. We pulled off the lid, scooped Frankie out of the tea, and dropped him into the sippy cup.

Some of the supporting cast kids fanned Mrs. Flushcowski with their pieces of cardboard while Mrs. Kumar ran off to get the school nurse.

Finally Mrs. Flushcowski opened her eyes. She looked at Pradeep and shook her head. "I was wondering why you had a goldfish in a bag at rehearsal. Now I see that you have

been planning this prank all along." Then she bellowed, "Give me your *HAT*."

Pradeep bent down and Mrs. Flushcowski snatched the green Robin Hood cap with the long perfectly tilted feather from Pradeep's head. I've never seen Pradeep look so sad.

I stepped forward. "Mrs. Flushcowski, it wasn't Pradeep's fault . . ." I started to say, but then she leaned over and put the hat on *my* head.

"It's noble of you to stand up for your friend, Tom, but actions have consequences." I think she could tell that I didn't really get what that meant, so she added, "People have to pay for what they do."

"But what if they didn't do . . ." I began, as she took Pradeep's bow and quiver of arrows from him and handed them to me. Suddenly all the words in my head dried up. Normally there is an ocean of words in there, but now there wasn't a drop. All I could think was that *I* could be Robin Hood.

"I can't . . ." A few words dribbled out of my dry brain.

"You are the only one who *can*, Tom. All the rest of the cast have important . . . I mean, *more vocal* roles, and you are the only one who knows all the lines, from practicing them with Pradeep," Mrs. Flushcowski said.

She was right. I did know the lines. I knew the fighting with the sticks, I knew the hanging on the rope, and I definitely knew the shooting of the arrows. I could do this part. I could *be* Robin Hood. OK, so it wasn't actually Pradeep's fault that the bag fell on Mrs. Flushcowski, but maybe he could have stopped it from happening if he had even *looked* at me once when I was trying to warn him. Maybe this was *payment* for what he did.

Pradeep walked over to me. He took off the green tunic his mom had made him and handed it to me. "I . . . um . . . won't give you the tights, um. . . . Mom has a spare pair," he mumbled.

Sami stood next to him with Frankie in the sippy cup. I gave Sami a look that said, "Maybe we should get Frankie out of here?" She understood right away. She put Frankie behind her back and ran over to her mom, who was just coming back into the hall with the school nurse. The nurse headed straight over to Mrs. Flushcowski while Mrs. Kumar took Pradeep and Sami out to the dressing room. I heard her saying, "Why on earth did you bring that goldfish onstage? I'm so disappointed in you. What were you thinking, Pradeep?"

The nurse gave Mrs. Flushcowski a fresh (fish-free) cup of tea with sugar in it and in a couple of minutes, she was back in director mode.

"Let's take it from the top. Reset for Act One."

While we mopped up the mess, propped up the cardboard scenery, and got ready to start again, Mrs. Flushcowski sent all the high-school boys off for a break until the real show that evening. I saw Mark breeze out of the back door. He didn't look at all upset, which got me thinking. If his evil plan was to ruin the play, it had failed (even though it ruined things for Pradeep). If it was to bump off Frankie, then that had failed too. So why wasn't he angry? I didn't have time to think about it now though. I was Robin Hood, after all.

We ran the dress rehearsal without stopping. I remembered every line, every move, and I started to notice that people were looking at me differently. And by "looking at me differently" I mean they were actually looking *at* me, not through me like they usually did. Guards One, Two, and Three didn't push past me as if I wasn't there. OK, so they still pushed past me, but now at least they looked at me first. Ladies-in-Waiting One, Two, and Three giggled when I walked by, but in a good way, not a laughing-at-you kind of way. And Merry Men One, Two, and Three actually looked merry when I told them a joke. Best of all, when Katie Plefka sang "Greensleeves," she looked right at me. I didn't like the song as much as Frankie did, but no one had sung to me since I was, like, three years old. I liked this feeling.

Because we had to start over, the dress rehearsal finished late and we barely had time to get fixed up again before the actual performance started. Sami ran over and gave me her sippy cup, which still had Frankie safe inside. Then I went to the dressing room and put on the full Robin Hood outfit for the first time. I looked at myself in the mirror. I *was* Robin Hood. Frankie

even gave me a little zombie goldfish smile. I knew he'd like the outfit 'cause it was green.

But there was something not right.

A funny feeling in my stomach. As if a load of millipedes were having a fight scene of their own in there.

CHAPTER 8

LIGHTS, CURTAIN, ZOMBIE!

People were starting to come into the hall and take their seats for the show.

I could see Mom at the back as I peeked through the curtain. She waved in that bigger than necessary, embarrassing way that only parents can do. Mrs. Kumar and Sami were there too. But not Pradeep. I guess he couldn't face coming.

I still had Frankie in the sippy cup. There was no sign of Mark now, but I knew he'd be back soon to run the special effects. I had to find a safe place to put Frankie. I looked around and saw that there were lots of red fire buckets full of sand backstage. I could dump the sand and fill one with water for Frankie. And if there was a fire, I could always scoop Frankie out and use the bucket to put out the fire. So technically it would still be a fire bucket. I put Frankie in a bucket and waited backstage to go on in my first-ever starring role. Everything was good.

So why couldn't I shake the millipedes kickboxing in my guts?

I peeked out from behind the curtain one more time and saw Pradeep slide into a seat next to Sami. He immediately looked up and shot me a look that said, "I've been a jerk. I'm really sorry. All the attention went to my head. This isn't your fault. Good luck as Robin

Hood—you'll be great." Then he gave me a double thumbs-up and added, "Oh yeah, and watch the arrows in Scene Three—they can be a bit tricky." That was the biggest look-message Pradeep had ever shot me and I understood every single word.

Then I got it.

I stood in the dark backstage and thought, *I know what that millipede feeling is. It's my conscience saying that I'm a terrible friend.*

Pradeep was my best friend. He had got the role of Robin Hood fair and square. I understood how he felt when everyone made him feel special, because it had just happened to me. My head had started to get a little bit big too.

I had to find a way to get Pradeep back onstage, and fast.

The lights went down and the opening music started. Then I heard two sounds that I never expected to hear together. I heard the sound of "Mwhahahaha, sucker!" coming from right above my head, and the sound of a fire bucket filled with water bumping across the floor.

Frankie had heard Mark's laugh and was after him to get revenge!

CHAPTER 9

ROBIN HOOD AND HIS ZOMBIE FISH

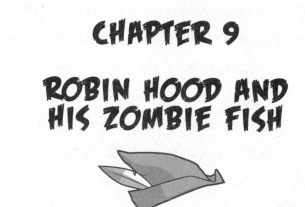

The audience started clapping and I could see the curtain swish as Mrs. Flushcowski walked in front of it to center stage.

"Thank you, everyone, for that spontaneous eruption of applause," she said.

I shook the image away. I had to concentrate. Mark and Frankie were both backstage somewhere, which meant only one thing. Trouble!

"I would like to announce that we have an esteemed guest with us this evening. From the hit television show *Talent or No Talent*, judge and creator Solomon Caldwell!"

The audience applauded again and I could hear a voice from the audience mumbling, "Thank you, thank you. It's a pleasure."

"Now, without further ado," said Mrs. Flushcowski, "I give you *Robin Hood*."

The curtain rose and the lights came up on the stage to show me and some Merry Men stick-fighting.

Then Merry Man One said, "There is a group of rich travelers approaching. Shall we let them pass or make them pay?"

"Their jewels will buy food for the starving poor," I said. "Let us hide. They won't see us in all this fog."

That was the cue for the backstage crew to start the smoke machine. Fake fog rolled onto the stage. I looked over and saw Mark standing by the machine with an evil grin on his face.

The kids dressed as rich travelers came out led by two kids dressed as a horse while the Merry Men and I hid behind some cardboard trees.

While the travelers and the horse were saying their lines (yes, even the back end of the horse had more lines than the baker), I looked around to see if there was any sign of Frankie.

In the audience, Sami was bouncing up and

down in her seat in the classic way kids all over the world let you know that they have to go to the toilet.

Pradeep got up to take her and they went out the back.

I heard my cue—the line that comes before mine in the play: "I guess that villain Robin Hood isn't about!"

We all jumped out from behind our trees and stood in front of the horse.

"You shall not pass until you give us all your gold!" I shouted.

Then my eye caught a glimpse of white from the side of the stage. Mark was putting on his white Evil Scientist lab coat. He was up to something, but what?

"The sheriff will know of your treachery, Robin Hood," the rich traveler said, and handed me a bag of chocolate money.

I looked past the offstage traveler. Mark took a test tube out of his pocket and poured some liquid into the smoke machine. The fog started to get thicker and thicker.

"I only rob the rich to give to the poor," I said, coughing, and handed the bag to one of the Merry Men. "Take this to the village."

By now I could barely see the Merry Man to hand him the bag. The fog was rolling out over the audience too. I put my hat over my mouth and nose and held my breath. Then I noticed the

rich travelers and the Merry Men were all falling asleep onstage. I looked out into the audience. They were all fast asleep too. Some of them were even *snoring*.

I dropped down low to the floor where the air was clearer. I remembered that from our fire safety drill. But I never thought I'd have to use it to avoid sleeping gas!

CHAPTER 10

SWEET DREAMS, EVIL PLANS

Mark was wearing a small gas mask that he had pulled out of his jacket pocket.

He walked onstage and looked out into the audience.

"Result!" he said, but in a mumbly way so it sounded like, "Meesulmt!"

"What did you say, Mark?" I said, but because I was talking through my Robin Hood hat it came out like, "Muut mid moo may, Maak?"

"Mang om," he mumbled, and stepped backstage to turn off the smoke machine. Then he picked up some of the cardboard that the cast had used to fan the air for the rope-swinging scene and wafted the fog away from the stage and out into the audience.

"I *said*, 'Result, moron,'" Mark said, taking off his mask. "That should be enough sleeping gas to keep 'em out for a bit."

I slowly took the hat away from my mouth and took a cautious breath. It seemed safe now. "Sleeping gas? Why?"

"I needed to—" Mark started to say, but I interrupted.

"You needed to knock them all out so they wouldn't stop you from getting Frankie?"

"No, I—" Mark started again.

"You needed to knock them out so that you could somehow make them all be your zombie fish slaves like when you tried to zombify the whole school last term?"

"Been there, done that," Mark scoffed.

"You needed them all unconscious so you could take over their minds and make them *all* go after Frankie?"

"No, but that sounds cool. Maybe next time," Mark said.

"Then why?"

"Duh? I needed to knock out Solomon Caldwell. The rest were just for fun. They do all look pretty stupid now that they're snoring and drooling." Mark did his Evil Scientist laugh. "You and the other moron gave me the idea with all this Robin Hood stuff you've been doing. Rob the rich—Solomon Caldwell—and give to the poor: me."

"I don't get it. You're going to rob Solomon Caldwell?" I said. "What are you going to take?"

"I'm gonna get him to make me the winner of *Talent or No Talent*. Then I'm gonna take the prize money. Easy."

"So your evil plan before wasn't to ruin the play? Or to kill Frankie?" I asked.

"No," Mark mumbled. "I can't kill the fish yet. I still need him. I caught him and was trying to tie him up out of the way in the rigging when

I accidentally knocked down Pradeep's stupid rope and dropped the moron fish. Still, it was pretty fun to see your moron friend get the blame."

Mark grabbed my wrists and tied them behind my back with some patented Evil Scientist wrist ties from his pocket. I really don't know why Mom keeps letting him order stuff from that Evil Scientists-R-Us catalog. "I gotta get on with my evil plan now, ya know, before everyone wakes up." He grinned.

"I don't get it. What do you need the money for?" I said.

"I need a lair," Mark said.

"A lair?"

"An Evil Scientist lair where I can have, like, a shark tank or a pit of crocodiles or something. Every Evil Scientist has got to have a lair. Mom won't buy me one, so I've gotta find the money some other way. It's her fault really," he said.

"But even if you get on the show, you're not gonna win. What's your talent?"

"I don't need a talent, even though I am pretty sick at rapping. I've got a goldfish that can make the judges *and* the public vote however I want. Starting with Solomon Caldwell."

He picked up the fire bucket from the side of the stage and showed me Frankie floating on the surface of the water.

"You've killed him!" I shouted, and pulled at my wrist ties.

"Relax, moron. He wouldn't be much good to me dead. At least, not yet," he said, and laughed again. "I put a couple of drops of the sleeping mixture into the water. He's out like a baby." He looked at Frankie. "A really ugly baby."

Mark tied a piece of string to Frankie's tail and carried him over to the front row where Solomon Caldwell was snoring away.

"Wakey, wakey, Solomon," he said, tapping his face with the wet goldfish.

"Leave Frankie alone!" I shouted. "He needs to go back in the water."

As Solomon started to come around, Mark swung Frankie back and forth in front of his face like a pendulum. Frankie was still really sleepy-looking, but his eyes fell open as he swung, and in seconds Solomon Caldwell was mumbling, "Swishy fishy!" and staring at the wall and up Mark's left nostril. Once Solomon was hypnotized, if Frankie didn't put a thought in his head and control him . . . Mark  could. Frankie was still too groggy though. His eyes fluttered closed.

Just then I heard a really faint owl call, and this was *definitely* a place where there shouldn't be any owls. Pradeep! I looked around.

Pradeep was backstage. His finger was in front of his mouth. Sami was with him. He motioned for her to *shhh*. Then he looked at me and gave a thumbs-up.

I kept one eye on Mark in the audience as he spoke to Solomon Caldwell. "When you wake up, you will make the first person you see a finalist on *Talent or No Talent*," he said in a very slow, relaxing voice. "I will hypnotize the other judges with the fish too. And everyone watching TV! I *will* be the winner of the big cash prize."

I kept the other eye on Pradeep and Sami. That wasn't easy without getting pretty dizzy.

All this time Frankie was still hanging by his tail. He couldn't survive out of water much longer!

Pradeep whispered something to Sami. Then he climbed up on the rigging above the stage. He started unwinding a curtain rope that was wrapped around a pole.

Mark turned back to me. "That was sooo easy," he said. He looked at his watch. "I've got a minute before the sleeping stuff wears off. I gotta make sure when Solomon Caldwell lays eyes on me, I look like a star."

He chucked Frankie in the bucket with the sleeping mixture and stomped offstage.

CHAPTER 11

A DRAMATIC SHOWDOWN

As soon as Mark was gone, Sami raced over from where she was hiding at the side of the stage. She was holding a quiver—you know, the bucket thing that holds arrows—which she had filled with water. She scooped up Frankie and dropped him inside. As soon as his gills touched the fresh water, he started to come around. He looked up at Sami and in a second she had the zombie stare again. She leaned the quiver up against my back.

"Swishy fishy snap, snap," she whispered, and then crawled offstage and hid behind a curtain.

"Snap, snap?" I whispered back, but she was already gone.

Then I heard a splash and felt a wet scratching against the wrist ties around my hands. Then another splash and then the scratching again. It took me a moment to realize that Frankie was jumping up and gnawing at the ties with his jutting, jagged, rotten teeth.

I looked up at Pradeep and shot him a look that said, "I'm nearly ready to do something, are you?" Then Pradeep leaned down and gave me the double thumbs-up sign (which almost made him fall off the rigging). Frankie jumped up one last time and with his final nibble, I could feel the ties fall from my wrists.

Right then Mark came striding out onstage with a hoodie on under his Evil Scientist lab coat, his hair gelled into spikes, and wearing dark sunglasses. He struck a pose.

"I look mega-cool, moron. Just like a winner of *Talent or No Talent* should." And he laughed a loud Evil Scientist laugh as he walked across the stage back toward Solomon Caldwell.

I was free, but I couldn't let Mark know. While his back was turned, I reached around on the floor and grabbed a couple of suction-cup arrows and a bow that one of the Merry Men had dropped when he fell asleep. I put the arrows in with Frankie and then slipped my hands and the bow behind my back so I still looked tied up, while Mark strode around onstage directly in front of Solomon Caldwell.

Suddenly the audience started to yawn and moan. The kids onstage rolled over and opened their eyes. People looked groggy and confused. While everyone was yawning and stretching, Sami snuck down off the stage and hid under

Solomon Caldwell's seat. She was clutching the baker's hat from my old costume.

I shot her a look that said, "What are you doing? Get back!"

She responded with a look that either said, "I'm getting into the prime position for temporarily incapacitating Solomon Caldwell so he can't look at Mark, thereby helping to keep Frankie out of danger" or "Me help swishy fishy go swish!" It was hard to tell which.

Mark smirked and posed right in front of the snoozing *Talent or No Talent* creator. "Now I just gotta do my Evil Scientist rap," he said with a grin.

I knew I had to act fast. I jumped up, slinging the quiver onto my back and pulling a suction-cup arrow out. I aimed my bow carefully. I hoped all my shooting-arrows practice with Pradeep would pay off. I crossed my fingers for luck, but then I remembered that you can't shoot an arrow with crossed fingers, so I uncrossed them again. Then I let go of the string.

The suction-cup arrow flew right into the back of Mark's hoodie, making him whip around to face me.

I heard a gasp from the audience and looked out. They were mostly awake now and looking confused. Robin Hood was fighting with an Evil Scientist? This was not even in the cartoon version!

"Too late!" Mark laughed as Solomon Caldwell began to open his eyes.

Mark started to rap:

*"People say I'm bad, they don't know the plan,
I'm worse than bad, I'm well evil, man . . ."*

This was *much* worse than I feared.

"Now, Sami!" I yelled, and Sami jumped out from under the seat with the baker's hat in her hands. She leaped onto Solomon's back and pulled the hat down over his head, covering his eyes before he could look at Mark.

"No!" Mark shouted. Then I heard a kind of mash-up between a Tarzan yell and a squeal of terror. It was Pradeep as he swung down from the rigging on a rope. He bashed into Mark and knocked him over.

Then one of the Merry Men shouted, "Robin, you have angered the sheriff!"

I guess he thought the show must go on even if it had completely changed direction since his nap.

Mark looked over at the kid and then at me. "Yeah!" Mark growled. "You shouldn't have done that, morons." He grabbed a fighting stick from Merry Man Number Three and came at me. He was much too close for me to fire an arrow, and other than those, I was unarmed.

I kinda got the feeling that "unarmed" was what was about to happen to me too.

CHAPTER 12

ZOMBIE'S GOT TALENT

In the audience, Solomon Caldwell was groggily trying to get the baker's hat off his head, but without much luck. The people sitting next to him were looking at him in confusion, probably trying to work out if this was also part of the show.

Pradeep grabbed a fighting stick and threw it to me. Then he grabbed another one from Friar Tuck and we both stepped toward Mark.

Mark's face throbbed red. He swung at both of us. Pradeep and I were quick, but Mark was strong. He swiped at me and knocked my Robin Hood hat clean off my head. That was close!

He swung at me again, knocking my stick out of my hands and into the wings. Then he turned to Pradeep and was pulling back, ready to swing, when I flung the fire bucket of water at him. His foot stomped right into it and he lurched to the side with one foot stuck fast. Water sloshed out all over him and the stage.

"Stupid morons!" he shouted. "You still can't stop me!"

Mrs. Flushcowski was desperately flicking through the play script on her lap. "But none of this is what we rehearsed," she squeaked. She looked at the stage and then at the audience. She still seemed a bit dazed from the sleeping gas. "And why is Solomon Caldwell playing the baker?" She seemed close to tears.

Just then, Mark grabbed Pradeep's stick and snapped it in two across his leg. He jumped down off the stage with the fire bucket still on his foot and clanked toward Solomon Caldwell, who was sleepily tugging on the baker's hat. I knew

what I had to do.

I pulled another suction-cup arrow out of the quiver on my back, but nearly dropped it when I saw that Frankie was clinging to the arrow with his front fins.

"Frankie, let go!" I shouted, but Frankie shook his fishy head. "Please. I'll only get one shot. If I miss, you could end up splatted on the wall."

Pradeep was standing next to me. "You have to," he said, and put the Robin Hood hat back on my head. "He can do it. And so can you, Tom." He looked out into the audience. "I mean . . . Robin, thou must shootest the arrow. It is your destiny!"

(I know Pradeep stole that last line from *Star Wars* instead of *Robin Hood*, but it suited the moment.)

Mark had reached Solomon's seat. He grabbed the hat and pulled it off, but Sami clamped her hands over Solomon's eyes and wouldn't let go.

"Swishy fishy say, 'Ptwwwwwwwwwwwwt!'" she said, and blew a raspberry at Mark.

It was now or never. I pulled back on the bow and fired the arrow *and Frankie* at Mark's face!

"Evil Scientist, you are *so* thwarted!" I yelled.

Mark turned and the suction-cup arrow hit him on the forehead and stuck there.

As soon as it hit, Frankie clung onto the arrow with his front fins and started fish-slapping Mark around the face with his tail.

"Get him off! Get the moron fish off me!" Mark yelled.

Pradeep stepped forward. "That rogue is now our prisoner. Get him!" Pradeep looked at the confused-looking Guards and Merry Men and Rich Travelers and even the horse. "Get him!" he repeated with a yell.

The cast jumped down into the audience and dragged Mark onstage while he was still trying to swat Frankie off his face.

The whole hall was going crazy. People were shouting. The audience was confused. The kids onstage didn't know what was going on, and no one, not even me, could get Frankie to stop fish-slapping Mark.

Mrs. Flushcowski had turned so pale that I thought she would keel over at any second. I suddenly had an idea of how to calm everyone down.

I went up onstage and whispered to Katie Plefka, who had been fanning Lady-in-Waiting Number Three with a bit of cardboard after she fainted when I fired the fish arrow. Katie nodded, walked to the center of the stage, and started to sing.

When
the first
notes hit
Frankie's ears,
he stopped
fish-slapping
Mark, jumped
into the water-
filled quiver
I was holding
out to him,
and started to sway to the music. The audience
went quiet. Sami gently uncovered Solomon
Caldwell's eyes and sat on the floor next to his
chair, rocking to the music. Solomon looked
straight at the stage. The Merry Men and the
Guards quietly tied up Mark with some of his
own Evil Scientist wrist ties while the rest of the
cast sat and listened to Katie sing.

When Katie hit her last note, the audience
burst into applause.

Katie smiled (and I think I spotted her head grow a little bit, but not too much).

Pradeep and I walked over and stood on either side of her.

"Hooray for Maid Marian!" I shouted.

"Hooray for Robin Hood!" shouted one of the Merry Men.

"Hooray for them both!" shouted a Lady-in-Waiting.

I took off the Robin Hood hat and put it on Pradeep's head. The audience clapped.

"Wait, I have something to say!" Solomon Caldwell spoke in a loud clear voice. The audience fell silent.

He walked slowly to the stage.

CHAPTER 13

FRANKIE STEALS THE SHOW

"That is the most mesmerizing voice I have heard in years," he said, looking at Katie. "I would love for you to appear on *Talent or No Talent*."

The audience clapped again.

Right away Pradeep and I looked at Solomon Caldwell's eyes for signs he was zombified. But he wasn't mumbling and he definitely wasn't looking up anyone's nostril.

We shot each other a look that said, "Could Frankie have wiped Mark's orders from Solomon Caldwell's brain before he opened his eyes, or is Katie only getting on the show because Mark hypnotized Solomon?"

"That's not fair! You were supposed to pick me!" Mark shouted, wriggling to get free of his ties. "I was supposed to win *Talent or No Talent*! I was supposed to win the prize!"

Solomon Caldwell continued, "I didn't say she'd won. There are lots of talented people out there. But I think she deserves a chance. What do you all say?" He looked out to the audience, and they all cheered.

I looked at Pradeep again. "He's not zombified. This is for real!"

"And this girl certainly isn't the only talented one at this school either."

Mrs. Flushcowski started to get some color back into her cheeks.

"She isn't?" she said. "I mean, no, of course she isn't." She smiled at him.

"Mrs. Flushcowski, can I just say on behalf of the audience that this is the most original production of *Robin Hood* I have ever seen? I must admit the first part was a bit slow. I think

I even nodded off at one point? But I loved the casting of two Robin Hoods and them working together with the whole cast to defeat the, er, Evil Scientist. And involving the audience in the play like that? Wow! Although I would have liked to have seen more of the end."

Just then Frankie splashed up from the top of the quiver and waved his tail like he was taking a bow, except he wasn't all zombie fish anymore. He was back to friendly Frankie. Phew!

"The fish arrow certainly was surprising," Mrs. Flushcowski said. "Now I know what you were doing with the fish in the rehearsal," she whispered to Pradeep. "You were planning this big finale!" She looked at Frankie. "But how did you get stage makeup on the fish to make his eyes look green?"

Pradeep whispered back, "Goldfish contact lenses—the latest thing."

Mrs. Flushcowski, still looking a bit shaky,

took a bow with Frankie.

"As I said, this school's got talent," Solomon Caldwell said, and everyone clapped again.

Mrs. Flushcowski stood onstage between Pradeep and me. "I don't know what to say, boys. I'm not really sure what happened tonight, but I'm very sure about one thing." She took another of her dramatic pauses. "You both make perfectly marvelous Robin Hoods."

The curtain came down with Katie, Pradeep, Frankie, and I waving to the audience, Mrs. Flushcowski beaming with pride and the other kids in the show all jumping around saying what a cool night they'd had.

Mom came backstage just as I was pouring Frankie into a water bottle to take him home. She gave me a big embarrassing hug in front of everyone, but I let her get away with it just this once.

Then she went over to Mark. "I had no idea you were in Tom's play. You kept that a surprise. You made such a good villain that Mrs. Flushcowski wants to give you private acting lessons."

Mark shot me a look that said, "I'll get you for this, moron!" as Mom dragged him off to speak to Mrs. Flushcowski.

Mrs. Kumar was right behind Mom and was carrying a very sleepy Sami. She brushed Pradeep's hair out of his eyes. "Now, there is my little man with a big heart, not a big head." And she pinched his cheeks. He hates it when she does that, but he let her just this once. "I'll pull the car up outside, Pradeep. I don't think Sami can stay awake another minute. It was nice of you to let her be in the show though."

Sami waved over Mrs. Kumar's shoulder as she was carried out. "Bye-bye, fishy!"

I looked at Pradeep. "I didn't get to say, with all the actual fighting evil and all, but you were a really great Robin Hood."

"You too." Pradeep smiled. "Hey, do you want to build the Supremely Secret Message Chute tomorrow?"

"Cool," I said. "Oh yeah, and I have to teach you our new game. Frankie and me are so gonna trounce you at Splat, Splosh, Grrr."

Just then Mrs. Flushcowski and Solomon Caldwell came over.

"I do hope that you boys will come back and star in next year's school play," Mrs.

Flushcowski said, "I haven't been that excited by a performance since I played 'Third Woman with Sword' in *Zelda, Warrior Woman*."

"I've heard so much about your act with the fish arrow too. If you ever want to do it on the show, just give me a call. You've *both* got talent." Mr. Caldwell smiled his Hollywood smile and handed Pradeep his card.

Pradeep and I looked at each other. We exchanged looks that said, "Naaaaah," then turned to Mrs. Flushcowski and Mr. Caldwell and said, "Naaaaah," out loud.

Then Pradeep added, "I mean, no thanks. Tom and I think we should retire from showbiz now. We never realized theater was so dangerous."

"Yeah," I agreed, and Pradeep and I both looked over at Frankie being rocked to sleep in his water bottle by Katie Plefka. "Besides, Frankie would always steal the show."

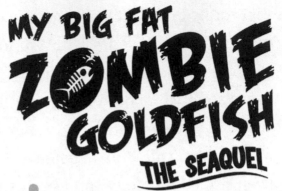